W9-COP-816

"You certainly know how to tempt a girl."

Kate said it enthusiastically as her eyes fell on the fresh bread, orange juice and a dish of yogurt.

There was a glint in the gray eyes that met hers and Alexander's wide mouth twitched. "You could have fooled me," he observed, "but I'm glad my professional skills have succeeded where my charm has so clearly failed."

Helena Dawson, a British writer, lives in Kent with her husband. They have three grown-up sons. She says she began her writing career relatively late in life by first entering a short-story contest, and then one for novels. She didn't win either one, but an interview with a senior editor afterward resulted in her first published novel. She now spends part of every day writing, but is also involved in village affairs. Her main interests are music and painting, and she sings with the local choral society.

WEB OF FATE
Helena Dawson

Harlequin Books

TORONTO • NEW YORK • LONDON
AMSTERDAM • PARIS • SYDNEY • HAMBURG
STOCKHOLM • ATHENS • TOKYO • MILAN
MADRID • WARSAW • BUDAPEST • AUCKLAND

If you purchased this book without a cover you should be aware that this book is stolen property. It was reported as "unsold and destroyed" to the publisher, and neither the author nor the publisher has received any payment for this "stripped book."

Original hardcover edition published in 1992
by Mills & Boon Limited

ISBN 0-373-17137-4

Harlequin Romance first edition May 1993

WEB OF FATE

Copyright © 1992 by Helena Dawson.
All rights reserved. Except for use in any review, the reproduction or utilization of this work in whole or in part in any form by any electronic, mechanical or other means, now known or hereafter invented, including xerography, photocopying and recording, or in any information storage or retrieval system, is forbidden without the permission of the publisher, Harlequin Enterprises Limited, 225 Duncan Mill Road, Don Mills, Ontario, Canada M3B 3K9.

All the characters in this book have no existence outside the imagination of the author and have no relation whatsoever to anyone bearing the same name or names. They are not even distantly inspired by any individual known or unknown to the author, and all incidents are pure invention.

® are Trademarks registered in the United States Patent and Trademark Office and in other countries.

Printed in U.S.A.

CHAPTER ONE

'FOR goodness' sake look where you're going, can't you?' Kate snapped. She glared at the two girls who pushed past her, tripping over the flight bag at her feet.

'Sorry, I'm sure!'

They nudged one another and giggled, eyeing a knot of lads lounging at the foot of the escalator a few yards away.

'Bit toffee-nosed, aren't we?' one of them remarked loudly to her companion as they flounced away, still giggling. 'Who does she think she is, anyway? Bet she's a teacher!'

Kate stared angrily after their retreating backs, irritated by their charmless behaviour and even more by the knowledge that somewhere, deep down, she actually envied them their heedless insouciance.

They weren't, clearly, eaten up by a sense of craven panic at the prospect of what lay ahead. For all they cared they might have been waiting to catch a bus.

Kate glanced up at the indicator board again, uncertain whether to be glad or sorry the information had not changed since she had arrived at the airport a couple of hours ago only to discover her flight was considerably delayed. Time had ceased to have any meaning in this traveller's no man's land, and her dread of flying had numbed her senses so much that she couldn't even summon up the energy or the determination to cut her losses and go home, and give up the whole idea of this trip altogether. After all, it had been foisted on her in the first place and by Liz, of all people, her friend whom she thought she could trust and who *knew* how much she hated flying.

How had she let herself be bullied into agreeing to go away, and just now, too, when the business was on the verge of an exciting expansion?

Kate picked up her bag and placed it on her lap, unconsciously wrapping her arms round it to hug it to her as she thought back to that evening last week when Liz had presented her with the *fait accompli* of an airline ticket already booked and paid for.

'You need a break, love,' her friend had told her firmly. 'You'll be fit for nothing if you go on as you are now. When did you last have a good night's sleep?'

She had peered at Kate closely. 'I hardly like to mention it, but you've got great rings under your eyes, and they're not good for business,' she'd added lightly, knowing full well that Kate's exhausted appearance had little if anything to do with the extra hours both girls were putting in before the opening of their second boutique.

'But I don't——' Kate had begun, but Liz had forestalled the familiar protestations.

'I know you don't like flying,' she acknowledged, 'but I've thought of that, too.'

She had rummaged in her bag and brought out a small white envelope which she held out to Kate.

'I know it's probably not ethical, but I got Ian to give me these for you. What's the point of having a doctor brother if you don't make use of him?'

'What are they?'' Kate had enquired doubtfully, turning the packet over in her fingers.

'Tranquillisers. There are only four, and they're very mild. Ian assured me about that. So you'll have two for the outward journey, and two for coming home—if you want to come home, that is. You wait till you see the house. You'll probably want to stay there for ever—start a new life and put everything else behind you.'

By 'everything', of course, Liz had meant Michael, but now was not, definitely not, the time to let her thoughts even begin to stray in that direction...

Kate's fingers tightened convulsively round her bag and brought her with a jolt back to the present. She must pull herself together. It was ridiculous sitting here, alternately brooding and panicking. Best to sacrifice this seat and fill in the time by getting a coffee.

Standing a few yards away was a young woman about her own age with a small baby in her arms, and Kate beckoned her over.

'You sit here—your need is definitely greater than mine.'

'If you're sure...?' The girl smiled gratefully, but hesitated before depriving Kate of her precious seat.

'Quite,' Kate assured her. 'I'm going for a coffee. Is there anything I can get you?'

'That's very kind of you, but I'm OK, thanks. My husband's over there somewhere with our little boy.'

She settled the baby comfortably and expertly on her lap. 'Have you got a family?' she asked, maternal contentment positively shining on her face.

'No,' Kate said, stooping to pick up her flight bag. 'No, I'm on my own.'

She smiled briefly and moved away, then turned on a sudden impulse to look back at the two of them, the girl talking softly to her infant, who was beaming back, secure in its mother's love even in these strange and noisy surroundings.

What must it be like to have a baby? Kate wondered suddenly with something suspiciously like an ache of longing, almost of jealousy, instantly suppressed. To be totally responsible for the well-being, even the survival, of another human individual—as Carol was going to be.

Anguish stopped her in her tracks and she closed her eyes for a second before pulling herself together quickly to elbow her way through the crowds. Maybe motherhood would suit Carol, but it certainly wasn't for her. Her own future lay in quite different directions, she'd always known that.

Standing in the coffee queue, she dragged her thoughts away from babies, and Carol, and even the alarming prospect of her imminent journey, and concentrated instead on all the thousand and one things that were still left to be organised before the new shop was due to open.

There was the publicity, for one thing. Liz's artistic flair might have contributed hugely to the success of their partnership, but she was the first to admit she wasn't the sternest of taskmasters when it came to overseeing other people's work, and Peter, the young graphic artist she had found to do their advertising material, certainly needed a firm hand to prevent him indulging his wilder flights of fancy—and to get him to deliver his designs on time.

Kate found a corner of a table and sat down with her coffee and a rather depressed-looking croissant, and opened her bag to find the folder of publicity material she'd brought with her to peruse. At least Liz couldn't stop her from doing *anything* useful while she was taking her enforced leave of absence.

'Oh!'

Someone knocked against her arm, and the whole sheaf of papers went flying under the table.

'Oh, really!' Kate burst out again, hardly bothering to look round to see who was to blame. 'Can't anyone in this place look where they're going?'

She slid off her seat and got down on her knees, anxious to rescue Peter's designs before people scuffed or trod on them, or, even worse, spilt coffee on them.

'I do apologise—careful, you're going to bump your head!'

Startled by the deep voice beside her, Kate had swung round, and felt a firm hand pressing down on her shoulder to prevent her braining herself on the sharp corner of the table.

'Come on, let me help you. It's the least I can do.'

A pair of strong, brown hands deftly collected up all the papers, then one of them stretched out to help Kate to her feet. Unwillingly she put her own into it, feeling hard, warm fingers close round her own as she scrambled up and found herself looking into a pair of humorous grey eyes.

'No harm done, I hope? As I said, I am sorry I was so clumsy. I don't make a habit of this sort of thing, I assure you, but I was forced into taking avoiding action on my own account—and just at the wrong moment, as it turned out.'

Kate realised that as the stranger smiled winningly down at her his fingers were still holding hers prisoner, and she snatched them away, her mouth tightening into a forbidding line.

'Thanks for your help,' she said frostily. 'As you have rightly observed, everything seems to be in order.'

She riffled through the papers and snapped the folder shut on them, then put it back into her bag as she resumed her seat to drink her rapidly cooling coffee.

'Not very appetising, is it?' the stranger remarked with irritating cheerfulness as he saw her expression of distaste and showing no sign of taking himself off and going about his own business. 'I always drink fruit juice myself. They can't do too much to ruin that.'

He reached out a long arm to pick up a beaker from the next table, and, as there was no adjacent seat free, perched nonchalantly on the edge of her table, forcing her to move her own cup out of the way.

'You don't mind, do you?' he enquired airily. 'Helps pass the time, having a chat, I always think. And time's something there's always too much of in these places. Oh, my name's Alexander, by the way, but my friends call me Alex.'

His wide, pleasant mouth twitched as his eyes rested quizzically on Kate's face, but she was not in the mood to respond to this all too blatant charm. She might be on her own, a fact which this Alexander had no doubt noticed, but she was no easy pick-up, as he was about to learn.

With a couple of swift gulps Kate drained her coffee, pushed the remnants of her croissant away and got up, meeting his surprised expression with a cool stare.

'There's no need for you to remain there, Alexander,' she told him, using his full name meaningfully. He was no friend of hers, nor likely ever to become one. 'I'm going now, so please, take my seat. You'll be much more comfortable.'

She stooped to pick up her bag, gave him a brief nod of farewell, and turned on her heel, mingling quickly with the shifting crowds in the concourse away from the coffee shop, just in case he had any idea of following her.

Once she was at what she thought was a safe distance she looked round, but she could see no sight of the stranger's dark head, and she allowed herself a small sigh of relief. She had enough to think about without coping with social small talk—at best. All the same, now she was safely out of harm's way she couldn't suppress a small twinge of remorse. She needn't have been quite so brusque. After all, he had stayed to help her pick up the papers, and he had had a very engaging smile...

Still, it was too late to worry about that now. She glanced up at the indicator board and her heart lurched, all thoughts of the grey-eyed stranger forgotten. At last her flight had been called and there was no going back now, not without a great deal of trouble, and offence to Liz, who had arranged this holiday for her.

'Don't be silly,' she chided herself silently as she marched off with a resolution she certainly didn't feel to the appointed gate. 'You've got your pill, if you get really panicky, and the flight will be over before you know it. Think of something else, think of the sun and the sea and Greece waiting for you.'

She had to admit it, now that the point of departure was actually upon her—the prospect of having two weeks entirely to herself was quite exhilarating. It would have been a terrible waste if she had refused Liz's offer...

'We meet again—that's nice! You're off to Athens too, then?'

With a sinking sense of the inevitable Kate turned to find Alexander smiling down at her, still irrepressibly cheerful and clearly in no way inhibited by her earlier brush-off.

'As you see,' she snapped, then brought herself up short, smitten by a recurrence of that twinge of guilt at her rudeness.

'I'm sorry,' she said stiffly, allowing her mouth to relax briefly into a semblance of a smile. 'I didn't mean...that is, yes, I am going to Athens. Then on somewhere else,' she added quickly, just in case he was tempted to get any unwelcome ideas.

'Oh—where...?' But the interested enquiries were swiftly cut off as Kate was carried along the passage and into the aircraft—no escape possible now—and struggled along to find her seat.

It was on the aisle, she'd made sure of that when she had checked in. Let those who actually enjoyed flying have the privilege of gazing out of the window at the earth thirty thousand feet below. She would bury herself in the thriller she'd bought and, when that palled, she could occupy her thoughts with a book of crosswords.

She was opening the luggage locker above her seat to stow her hand luggage away when she heard a voice behind her—a voice whose owner she didn't need to turn round to identify.

'Here, let me help you. It'll be easier for me, I'm taller.'

'I can manage quite well, thanks,' Kate assured him coolly. 'I'm quite used to travelling alone.'

She pushed her bag in and slammed the locker shut on it, only to have to watch him open it again to put his own bag in.

'No need to bite my head off,' the stranger who called himself Alexander said genially. 'It was an offer kindly meant, I assure you. I wasn't trying to cast aspersions on your ability to look after yourself. However, if you'll excuse me, I need to get past you into that seat there.'

To Kate's dismay the one he was indicating was the one next to hers, the centre one of the row of three.

'I'm sorry, you seem to be stuck with me for the journey,' Alexander commented not at all apologetically, then his grin changed into a grimace as he eased his tall frame into the seat.

'Designed by pygmies, these, aren't they? Thank goodness we're only going to Athens, not Hong Kong.'

Kate had her own reasons, which had nothing to do with her size, for wishing the flight to be as short as possible, and while Alexander was chatting to his other neighbour she rummaged in her handbag for the pill which she had been keeping for this moment and which she devoutly hoped would knock her out for the whole journey.

Then, even as her hand closed over the packet a cussed streak asserted itself, and the corners of Kate's mouth tilted with a flicker of grim humour. If this plane was destined to crash, a pill wasn't going to stop it. She wouldn't actually take one, not yet—just keep them handy, in case.

Some tenseness on her face must have been visible, in spite of her brave resolve, as Alexander turned back to her with a sympathetic smile.

'There's nothing to worry about, you know. I do this trip once a month, at least.'

Did this man miss nothing? Kate thought in mounting annoyance as she treated him to her coldest stare.

'I'm not scared,' she said icily, then, noting the dark eyebrows rise a fraction, added more honestly, 'Well, I suppose I am just a bit apprehensive. I know it's not rational, and these machines are as safe as the proverbial houses, but if there were another way of getting about the world...'

She shrugged then leant back in her seat, closing her eyes. She had already confessed more than enough to this man. Perhaps he would now take the hint that she wanted—needed—to be left in peace, but he seemed to have the sensitivity of a sledge-hammer.

'With me sitting beside you you won't need that pill you're still clutching to take your mind off your worries,' he told her airily. 'You might even become so fascinated by my conversation that you'd be wishing the flight were twice as long.'

'I doubt it,' Kate muttered from between clenched teeth. 'Look,' she went on, turning towards him and fixing him with what she hoped was a basilisk stare that would freeze the flow of words in his throat, 'I don't mean to be rude——' she felt her cheeks grow warm as his dark brows rose lazily over quizzically appraising eyes '—but I do really prefer my own company. I've a lot on my mind at the moment, and, as you've now discovered, I hate flying. All I want to do is block out everything around me till I've got where I'm going.'

She flashed him a brilliant smile, turned her head away again and shut her eyes. Surely no one, not even this persistently interfering man whom fate had thrust into her path, could fail to get *that* message?

To her relief it did seem that he had, as he made no further attempt to engage her in conversation and she was able to bury herself in her detective story during take-off without any further interruption from him; a while later she actually found her tense muscles relaxing, and her fingers uncurling on her lap, as she settled herself more comfortably into her seat. A strangely reassuring warmth seeped into her from the arm pressing gently against hers, and she knew she ought to move, but she was too sleepy... And as her head drooped, the man beside her smiled.

Kate came to with a jolt as the stewardess was announcing the arrival of the drinks trolley.

To her utter chagrin she discovered that her head was resting against Alexander's shoulder and she sat bolt upright, daring him to make some wisecrack at her expense, but all she heard was a soft voice asking whether she felt better now.

'Yes, thanks,' Kate replied shortly. She fumbled in her bag for a comb and mirror. As she'd feared, she looked a complete mess with flushed cheeks and dishevelled hair. She pulled a face as she repaired the damage as best she could, smoothing back her chestnut hair behind her ears, and touching up her lipstick.

'Very nice,' Alexander approved, 'and don't glare at me again. It doesn't suit you.'

He leant forward to peer more closely at her and Kate found herself gazing straight into his eyes, unable in this confined space to escape from his penetrating yet always gently humorous stare.

'Are you always so prickly, Miss...? Do you know, I still don't know your name.' He glanced quickly down at her left hand. 'It is Miss, is it? Or are you a Ms?' he grinned.

'Miss,' Kate told him with an irritable sigh. 'Miss Kate Penwarden.'

'Ah,' Alexander nodded with apparent satisfaction. 'Well, Miss Kate Penwarden, are you?'

'Am I what?'

'Always so prickly—unless you prefer to call it independent? Or is it travelling that brings out the women's libber in you, making you refuse offers of help or polite conversation—and I'm never anything but polite, I do assure you.'

For the briefest of moments Kate glimpsed what looked like a shadow cloud Alexander's open expression, and again she felt a pang of remorse flick through her. He was quite right. He had shown her nothing but courtesy, even if his manner was irritatingly extrovert, and all she had done was show him the cold shoulder, and with no good reason at all.

She managed a wan smile. 'I'm sorry,' she said stiffly. 'I haven't meant to be rude. It wasn't anything personal, but I am best left to myself at the moment. You know already I'm not the bravest of travellers...' She paused, then went on with a slight shrug, 'I have other things on my mind, too, and I'm not really in the mood to be jollied along.'

The arrival of the drinks trolley prevented Alexander from prolonging this discussion, and Kate deliberately turned away to speak to the stewardess, but almost before she had opened her mouth Alexander had forestalled her.

'This lady is going to share a bottle of champagne with me,' he said with a calm authority that took her breath away. 'And I'm sure you can find us one that is already chilled...?'

The stewardess smiled. 'Of course, sir, if you'll just wait a minute?'

'You do like champagne, I imagine?' Alexander enquired calmly of Kate, ignoring totally her outraged expression at his high-handed behaviour. 'It's easily the most effective tranquilliser I know, and the only way to start a holiday. You are on holiday, I presume, and not a business trip?'

'Yes,' Kate replied with a resigned sigh, knowing when she was beaten—temporarily, at least. 'I am on holiday. And I do like champagne. Thank you very much.'

The stewardess handed them two glasses, and Alexander raised his to Kate.

'To a happy holiday, then.'

Kate acknowledged the toast, and sat back in her seat to enjoy her drink, her spirits already lifting as Alexander had promised they would, she realised ruefully, and as he, too, leant back in his seat to stare sideways out of the window Kate found herself studying him covertly from beneath her deliberately lowered lashes. As she watched him, a mental picture of Michael slid before her to block out the dark head now angled away from her and hiding the grey, amused eyes which exuded such good-natured charm—a charm she had so resolutely kept at bay.

How different he was from Michael. Even his best friend, even she herself, couldn't have called him charming.

Confident, compelling, and domineering, too— Michael was all of those things and at the beginning he had been tender and generous, as well, Kate recalled sadly... and they had loved one another, there was no disguising that fact, however much she would have liked to. So what had gone wrong? How could he have betrayed her so cruelly, actually having an affair with someone else when he was still engaged to her, Kate— and still planning to marry her?

Instinctively the fingers of her right hand felt for the reassurance of Michael's diamond, but of course they found nothing. Her left hand was bare, with not a mark left from where her engagement ring had encircled her fourth finger for so long—three years and four months, her memory prompted her.

Her hands clenched into fists on her lap as she stared straight ahead of her, hurt anger creasing the smooth skin of her brow. No, don't even think of that, she told herself sternly. You must put all that behind you, and in any case this is definitely not the time to begin brooding.

She took another sip of champagne, her eyes refocusing on Alexander's dark head which was still turned away from her as he chatted to his other neighbour, who seemed to be pointing out some landmark on the earth miles below.

Such very black hair he had, she mused idly, springing and vital as it curled into his strong neck. Could he perhaps be Greek? There was some hint of accent in his deep voice, but those grey eyes—they weren't of Mediterranean origin, surely?

His brown hand was spread out on his thigh as he leant across to peer out of the window, and for an instant Kate felt an insane desire grab hold of her to reach out and cover it with her own.

Appalled, she shrank back into her seat. What was she thinking of? There must be no question of any sort of involvement with any other man, least of all this one. Her work must be the whole centre of her life now, and it would remain that way. She wasn't cut out for romance, or love either. Michael had not minced his words when he'd told her as much.

To her horror she felt tears pricking her eyelids, and she bent her head to brush them away quickly. The last—the very last—thing she wanted was for the man called Alexander to see her crying. Mercifully, he was still preoccupied with the view, apparently noticing nothing, and Kate was able to pull herself together by the time their meal arrived.

'Have some more champagne,' Alexander invited her, filling her glass before she could either accept or refuse. 'If nothing else, it should help make the meal more palatable. Airline food can scarcely be called one of life's great gastronomic experiences, can it?'

Kate laughed, in spite of herself, and watched Alexander's eyebrows shoot up in mock astonishment.

'You *laughed*, Miss Penwarden. There must be something even more to this bottle than meets the eye. Are you sure you're feeling all right—not too intoxicated?'

He took a sip from his own glass and shook his head sagely. 'No. It tastes quite normal to me. But something's happened to you. It must be the altitude.'

He nodded to himself as he dabbed unenthusiastically at a bright pink concoction that called itself taramasalata.

Kate sighed and began eating her own meal. 'You asked me if I was always prickly. Can I ask you something?'

'Anything. Ask away. It gives me more pleasure than I can say just to hear you talking to me.'

'Are you always so frivolous? Aren't you ever serious? This constant cheeriness must be very wearing to your friends.'

'Frivolous? I'm not frivolous. Whatever gave you that idea, Miss Penwarden? I simply thought you needed cheering up, but if you prefer I could discuss the ethics of genetic engineering, or the return to Greece of the Elgin Marbles. Or maybe I could interest you with my views on the decline of the film industry? You only have to say.'

He took another mouthful of salad, then laid down his fork with a comic expression of despair as he turned once again to face Kate.

'We could even talk about you, Miss Penwarden,' he suggested lightly, 'and what it is that's bringing you to Athens and beyond on your own.'

Kate sighed, refusing to be drawn. 'There you go again. You're not really serious, you're still only making fun of me.'

Alexander shook his head. 'I'm not, as it happens, but you wouldn't mind if I were, would you? You thought you did, but not any more.' He leant across and peered closely into her face then nodded with satisfaction.

'That tense look's gone from behind your eyes, and there were little lines just there...'

A gentle finger touched her forehead just between her eyebrows, then it withdrew as quickly as it had come and the potentially dangerous moment passed, leaving Kate staring confusedly down at the tray in front of her. She ought to be cross at Alexander's unasked-for caress, and relieved it had lasted so brief a moment, but she couldn't deceive herself that it was mere maidenly outrage that made her pulses beat fractionally faster than normal.

She sensed Alexander's eyes flick towards her, gauging her reaction, but she kept her own gaze resolutely on the meal, for which her appetite was diminishing rapidly, not wishing either to give anything away or to encourage him any further. He was still a stranger in spite of their enforced proximity, and that was how he must remain.

She glanced at her watch, pleased to discover how much of the journey had already passed, and rather to her chagrin she had to admit to herself that Alexander had helped her forget her usual terrors. She wasn't listening for each change in the engine noise to herald imminent disaster, and for that much at least she must be thankful. It was almost a pity he wouldn't be accompanying her on the short trip from Athens to Kalamata.

'Oh, no!'

Kate sat up with a jolt that almost spilt the coffee she'd just accepted from the stewardess, and which made Alexander turn to her in concern.

'What's the matter? Just remembered you've forgotten something? Some important papers, perhaps?'

Kate shook her head in agitation. 'No, nothing like that, and in any case I'm not...' She broke off and ran her hands through her hair. 'That delay at the airport, before we took off...' She waved her hand helplessly. 'I'll have missed my connecting flight. The other plane will be sure to have left long before we land. There was only an hour to spare as it was.'

Somehow this seemed the final straw. She hadn't wanted to make this trip in the first place, and, far from getting rid of the stresses Liz had claimed she was suffering from, it was aggravating them by the minute.

Normally she would be able to take this sort of small inconvenience in her stride. Goodness knew, she came up against them often enough in her business life, so why should she suddenly feel so vulnerable and unable to cope?

She sank her chin in her hand, then became aware that Alexander was talking to her, softly now, and not in his usual deliberately cheerful tone.

'There's no need to worry, Kate. I'm sure we can fix up something—another flight, or a hotel, whichever seems the more convenient. Just tell me where you're heading, and I'll sort it out for you when we get to Athens.'

Some mulish streak—her own independent spirit reasserting itself, perhaps—clamped Kate's lips into a more determined line.

'No, I'll be fine, thanks.' She directed a bright smile towards him. 'It was just the sudden realisation that threw me for a minute. As you say, there must be plenty of hotels around, and they can't all be full, not at this time of year. I'll be fine, don't worry about me.'

The grey eyes that met hers were unexpectedly grave. 'If you don't want to tell me where you're heading, that's OK by me. There's no reason why you should, but I just thought if we were both heading in the same direction I could give you a lift, that's all. I shall be driving south, if that's any help?'

Kate didn't want to tell a downright untruth, but for some reason she couldn't fathom neither did she want to tell Alexander she was also going south from Athens. In any case, 'south' was a very vague term, and she had no wish to let Alexander's chivalrous impulse take him out of his own way.

At least that was the reason she gave herself for refusing his offer of help.

'I really shall be all right,' she assured him again. 'It's very kind of you to offer me a lift, but I'm sure things'll work out, and even if there isn't a flight for a couple of days, I can use the time to visit Athens, can't I?'

Alexander's eyes rested enigmatically on her face for a moment and Kate felt uncomfortably that he could see only too clearly through her prevarication and would think she was giving him a definite brush-off—again.

'If you're sure, then . . . but the offer's still open, until touch-down, anyway.'

The easy-going atmosphere between them had changed subtly now, and for the rest of the journey they hardly exchanged more than a few casual remarks as Alexander began to read a magazine, although, Kate noted surreptitiously, the pages turned no more quickly than those of her own book, which she had hoped would while away the remaining hour and keep her old anxieties from beginning to edge back into her mind.

What he was thinking, she couldn't guess, except that she had a sneaking suspicion that it might have something to do with independent-minded prickly career girls who insisted on rebuffing even the most sincere offers of help.

If he'd been a different sort of man she would almost have thought he had withdrawn into a shell of reserve— even that she had hurt him. But that was ridiculous. His sort used charm as a weapon, and if she had blunted it a little, well, tough luck. Who knew what a lift in his car would have led to, anyway?

Much better to keep him at arm's length and go her own way, whatever inconveniences she might meet along it. She could cope.

'You'll be all right, then?' Alexander asked when they had landed and were walking across to the airport buildings. 'You really don't want a lift? The offer's still there, you know.'

Kate shook her head firmly, making her chestnut hair swing round her face. 'No, thanks. I'm sure I can sort everything out. I'm quite used to looking after myself.'

'Mmm.' Alexander looked quizzically down at her. 'Well, you know best—but there's one thing I must say before we go our separate ways...'

He paused and the old humorous glint came back into his grey eyes. 'I don't know, you might bite my head off again... still, maybe it'll be worth the risk.'

They were in the queue for Passport Control now, forced close together by the crowd of travellers, and Kate had to tilt her head back to look up at him and now, when it was too late to go back on her decision, she felt a niggling regret that she hadn't agreed to accept his offer of a lift. There was, she had to admit, something very attractive about that smile, and maybe she had been unfair to suspect he might take advantage...

'A drachma for them?'

Kate came to with a start. 'Nothing... nothing at all.' She coloured slightly under Alexander's persistent gaze. 'What was it you were going to say?'

Alexander stooped over her, and with the press of people at her back she was unable to take any avoiding action, but she held his gaze with clear green eyes wide with anticipation.

'Just that now you've stopped being over-anxious and suspicious—not to say prickly,' he added with a grin, 'you really are very pretty, Miss Penwarden. Or even prettier, I should say.'

He turned then to have his passport checked, passed the time of day in fluent Greek with the officials, and, much to Kate's surprise and chagrin, disappeared quickly out of sight among the milling throng in the airport concourse.

Had that been his farewell? she mused, as she wandered off in search of her luggage. If so, it was very abrupt. She'd have expected something a bit more prolonged from him—unless he had decided to escape in expectation of a sharp reprimand for his compliment.

She couldn't help feeling just a little hurt, but wasn't that a bit hypocritical when she had been so offhand with him? Anyway, there was no time to brood on his odd behaviour. She must see to her own affairs and find out about her plane to Kalamata, or a hotel for the night.

'Ah, there you are. I thought I'd lost you.'

The familiar voice behind her made her swing round.

'Alexander! So you hadn't gone.'

'Gone without saying goodbye? That would hardly have been very chivalrous, would it? No,' he went on, giving Kate no time to comment, 'I took it on myself to make some arrangements for you. Here—let's find a quieter spot.'

With a hand under her elbow he guided her to a less busy corner where he fished in his pocket and handed her a slip of paper.

'Here's the time of your plane to Kalamata tomorrow—and there's no problem. There'll be a seat available.'

'Kalamata!' Kate exclaimed. 'But I never mentioned——'

'No, but your luggage did,' Alexander pointed out. 'Your label,' he went on, laughing gently at Kate's bemused expression. 'And there's a little hotel just up the road, round the corner. The Alexandros.' He pulled a face. 'Sorry about that, but I...I happen to know the manager. Anyway, it's quiet—relatively—and I took the liberty of booking you a room. If you're still sure you won't come with me—and your feminist tendencies aren't going to object too violently to having the arrangements made for you?'

Kate was too taken aback to make any objections and merely nodded weakly.

'Thanks—for fixing the room, I mean. And thanks too for the champagne, and for trying to cheer me up on the flight. I'm sorry I wasn't better company.'

She smiled up at him, then her eyes widened as without warning he bent and kissed her lightly on the cheek.

'Couldn't resist it,' he told her airily. 'Especially as it's my last chance. I don't suppose our paths will cross again, unless the Fates decree otherwise, but, if you should need anything, here's my card. There should always be someone there who knows where to get hold of me.'

He drew a wallet out of an inside pocket of his jacket and, as he opened it, Kate caught a glimpse of a photograph of a dark and pretty girl, smiling at the camera.

She felt a stab of disappointment that there was someone this important in his life, but almost as soon as she had registered this unwelcome reminder of her feminine susceptibility Alexander had closed his wallet again. She saw him frown, and deep lines appeared suddenly between his brows before his face cleared again as he held out his card.

'Alexander Dimitrakos,' she read, followed by an address in Athens.

'So, have a good trip, Kate,' he said. '*Kalo taxidi*.' Then, smiling at her over his shoulder he turned away and strode off soon to be lost to sight among the crowd, leaving Kate feeling unaccountably and uncharacteristically bereft.

CHAPTER TWO

THE Alexandros Hotel turned out to be a much grander place than Kate had envisaged from Alexander's description, and her room, adjoining a large bathroom, was quite luxurious, with a king-size bed—rather over the top for just one person, Kate thought, amused—a television, and a fridge full of a wide selection of bottles to suit any taste, however cosmopolitan.

'You have everything you need?' enquired the manager, who rather to her surprise had shown her up himself. 'I can have a meal sent up, if you wish?'

'No, thanks. I had something on the plane not long ago,' Kate told him.

'Then this evening, perhaps? The restaurant downstairs will be open at seven, and I can recommend our menu—unless you would prefer to go out? In which case, tell the receptionist and she will order you a taxi.'

Kate told the manager she would eat downstairs, which seemed to please him, and when he had gone she helped herself to an iced mineral water which she sipped ruminatively, unsure whether to be annoyed or flattered that Alexander had arranged for her to stay in this clearly not inexpensive hotel.

How did he know she'd want to stay somewhere like this, or even that she could afford to? He could at least have checked before he'd booked her in, she thought rather crossly, then, catching sight of herself in the mirror, she relented. He knew she was a businesswoman, and her designer suit, if nothing else, would have given him some clue about her financial circumstances, so in a funny sort of way it had been a com-

pliment, his assumption that she was well enough off
and sufficiently successful to be able to afford this hotel's prices.

She undressed and had a leisurely shower and slipped
into the towelling robe hanging behind the door before
lying back on the bed to make up her mind how to spend
the time before dinner.

There was nowhere to go, not round here, she'd seen
that in the short distance from the airport, and she felt
too lethargic to want to get a taxi into Athens; in any
case, it wouldn't be any fun sightseeing on her own.

She got out the book in which she had made so little
headway on the plane, but got hardly any further even
now, in the comparative quiet of her bedroom.

Each time she reached the foot of a page she realised
she hadn't really taken in more than half of what she
had read, and then, as though mocking her, she would
see a certain pair of grey eyes dancing over the print,
impeding her progress still further.

Drat the man! Kate flung the book down on the bed
to go and stand by the window, staring out at the un-
attractive concrete block of flats opposite.

How a nation which had built the Parthenon could
design such appalling buildings as those which crowded
in all around the hotel and lined the road into Athens
was beyond her imagining. Maybe she should have taken
that taxi ride after all to restore her faith in all things
Greek—or maybe, she thought slowly, she should after
all have accepted Alexander's offer of a lift...

Again she saw his face projected on the white wall of
her room as though the very Fates who had thrown them
together were determined to play games with her.

There was no rational explanation she could think of
for her feelings of indecision, making her act so out of
character. By now, in normal circumstances, she would
have been climbing the Acropolis and filling in every
spare minute with useful activity.

But how could a mere stranger exert such a disturbing effect on her, and in his absence, too? She knew she was never going to meet him again, so why go on even thinking about him? If she was feeling out of sorts it was far more likely to have something to do with the journey and the delay. After all, she had left home very early this morning...and all this on top of the break-up with Michael. She still had in no way come to terms with that.

Kate lay back on the bed, hoping to doze off, but sleep eluded her as she saw first Alexander's face, then Michael's, imprinted on her closed eyelids, and her thoughts went back with awful inevitability to that last dreadful evening when she'd confronted the man she'd thought for so long she would marry with her knowledge that he'd been having an affair, over several months, with his secretary.

In fact, the evening had been planned to fix—finally—a date for their wedding, only it hadn't turned out that way, Kate thought wretchedly, trying to blot from her mind the harsh words both of them had uttered in their anger and bitterness.

Kate had never imagined it could be possible to feel so humiliated and so furious at the same time.

'How *could* you?' she had stormed. 'Pretending you were away on a business trip to—where was it—Paris? Paris!' she'd repeated with a bitter laugh. 'Trust you to be original! What a cliché! And all the time you were having it off with Carol.' She had shaken her head in total disbelief before continuing, 'And then to come back to try and pin me down to a date for our wedding, as if nothing had happened, before going off again.'

Her eyes blazed with emerald fire. 'And now you have the nerve to expect me to forget it ever happened. An aberration, you called it. Well, it may have been an aberration as far as you were concerned, but it wasn't for me, nor, I suspect, for Carol, either.'

'Carol understood,' Michael had responded coolly, 'which is more than you ever did.'

He'd swung away to pace around the room. 'You wouldn't commit yourself to a date for our wedding, you wouldn't let me make love to you, let alone come and live with you—God, Kate, I'm not a saint, nor a hermit! I have needs, too, like any man, and when Carol...' He'd paused then, and dropped his eyes, unable to meet her outraged expression. 'There's something else you ought to know,' he began, before coming to a halt as though reluctant to continue.

'Go on,' Kate had said hollowly, already suspecting what was coming.

'Carol's going to have a child—my child.' Michael had had the grace then to look, if not ashamed, at least uncomfortable as he unleashed his bombshell and turned away to jingle his coins deep in his trouser pocket.

It was then that he uttered the words that were so wounding, Kate knew she'd hear them till her dying day.

'That needn't worry you, though, need it? You may have decided we wouldn't have a family, and I pretended to go along with it because I loved you, but I'd assumed when we were married you'd want a family of your own—our own—like any other normal woman. But you're not normal, are you? You've never agreed to fix a date for your wedding—your marriage to me—because you're married to your work, I see that now...and I hope you'll be very happy together, you and your boutique.'

Too stunned even to speak, Kate had stared at Michael in utter disbelief until finally, fighting to keep back her tears, she had twisted off her ring and handed it to Michael.

'I guess it's a good thing we've found out the truth about one another before it's too late,' she'd whispered, her voice hoarse with anguish. 'I hope you'll never know what it is to feel as betrayed as I do now. I wouldn't wish that on my worst enemy—not even on you.'

Michael had flinched and his voice had been low and not quite steady as he'd opened the door to leave her flat and walk out of her life for ever. 'I've never wanted anyone but you, Kate, but you forced me—us—into all this. It's quite clear to me there's no room in your life for me—nor anyone else either.'

The bitterness of their final exchange had rung in Kate's ears all that night and echoed down the days so that she could still hear it here, a whole month later and hundreds of miles away.

How could she ever have contemplated marrying a man capable of such treachery? And as for that last, final accusation—that she could never forgive. Michael, of all people, knew her reasons for her decision—not lightly taken, heaven knew—not to have children. How could he have used that weapon against her?

She closed her eyes in a steely resolve to shut out the whole of the scene replaying itself in her head, then sat up quickly to look at her watch. This was not the time, nor the place, to indulge in an orgy of self-pity.

Surely it was time for a meal? She'd go down and have the best meal the Alexandros could provide, and celebrate the start of the rest of her life with a bottle of their most expensive wine. Well, maybe half a bottle, she smiled wryly to herself as she locked her room behind her. She had no wish to add a hangover to her other problems.

The following morning Kate woke feeling surprisingly refreshed after a sounder sleep than she had had in weeks, and there was another surprise awaiting her when she asked for her bill.

'There is nothing to pay, madam,' the manager beamed broadly. 'All has been settled. I thought you must know.'

'Know? How could I know—and who on earth has paid the account? No one knew I was here...' Kate paused. 'No one,' she went on slowly, 'except...'

The manager's next words fulfilled her sudden suspicion.

'Kyrios Alexandros Dimitrakos has requested the account be sent to him. Of course, you know he owns this hotel?' he continued, still smiling. Clearly Alexandros was a popular employer.

Alexander... the Alexandros! Of course, she should have guessed there was some connection.

'I see,' she said rather dazedly, feeling the wind had been taken out of her sails. 'I'll thank him—Kyrios Dimitrakos, of course, and thank you, too, *kyrie*, for making me so welcome. The room was most comfortable, and it really was an excellent dinner last night.'

Excellent and, for Greece, very expensive, Kate thought smugly as she sat back in the taxi for the short drive back to the airport. Well, it served Mr Alexandros Dimitrakos right.

She smiled, half annoyed, half amused at the man's deviousness. If ever she should catch up with him again, she'd give him a piece of her mind for deceiving her like that, but at least his ploy had had the effect of sending her off on the next stage of her journey in higher spirits than she'd begun it yesterday, and she boarded the plane to Kalamata with barely a tremor, quelling, as she took her seat, a momentary pang of regret that her neighbour was an elderly Greek lady, not the tall, dark, grey-eyed stranger called Alexander who had humoured her ill-temper, found her a room in a hotel—his hotel...

Her hand stole to her cheek and her lips curved in a reminiscent smile at the memory of that gentle kiss, then she shook her head crossly. One thing Michael had taught her, at least, and that was that she was never going to allow herself to become attracted to any man, ever again.

None of them could be trusted, and she was going to see to it that all her energies and all her emotions would be centred entirely on building up her business.

But her emotions had other ideas when to her utter amazement she caught sight of Alexander's tall figure standing in the small airport building at Kalamata, obviously waiting for someone, to judge from the way his eyes were searching the crowd of incoming passengers.

He'd actually come to meet her, and after she'd been so definite about refusing his offer of help yesterday. But why hadn't he told her he was coming to Kalamata? Then she might have accepted his offer of a lift. Still, none of that mattered now. The main thing was that he was here.

'Alex!' she called out, standing on tiptoe and raising a hand to wave before she pulled herself together as she realised how over-eager she must look.

She dropped her hand and pushed her way through the crowd that separated them. 'Alexander!' she called when she was nearer. 'I'm here!'

Was it her imagination, or was there some hint of surprise on the handsome face that turned in her direction? But, if so, it vanished too soon for her to be sure, as a mischievous light glinted in the grey eyes that had had such an unsettling effect on her state of mind the day before.

'Did you sleep well, Miss Penwarden?'

'Very well, thank you, but——'

'No buts, Kate. I know what you're going to say, and I won't hear of it.'

'Won't hear of what?' Kate demanded rather pointlessly.

'Of you offering to pay. I know——' he spread his hands in mock apology '—maybe it was a bit underhand, but you needed a room, I own a hotel, so...what else could I have done?'

'Come clean?' Kate suggested airily.

'And suppose you hadn't wanted to stay there? I couldn't assume you'd be able to afford it, could I? In any case, please credit me with some honourable instincts. I know you think I'm just an irritatingly frivolous fellow——'

Kate flushed. 'I'm sorry. I shouldn't have said that. I wasn't quite myself yesterday.'

'But you are now?'

'Yes—thanks to your generosity...' She hesitated and her flush deepened. 'I do have to confess to having had a rather expensive meal last evening. Won't you even let me——?'

'Out of the question,' Alexander told her firmly. His eyes left her face then to scan the rest of the passengers off the plane, and his expression lightened as he caught sight of someone behind her.

'And now, if you'll excuse me, and I can't be of any further assistance to you...'

'Oh...no! Thanks.' Kate was rather taken aback, but hoped it didn't show. So it hadn't been she whom Alexander had come to meet. Then who...?

She said a rather brief farewell to Alexander who, though still courteous, was clearly distracted now and anxious to go and meet whoever it was he had been waiting for.

Kate collected her luggage and moved away towards the exit, then turned, her heart instantly plummeting to the floor as she watched Alexander, his face alight, walk quickly up to a girl—a dark, beautiful girl who flung her arms round his neck and kissed him warmly on the lips.

But it wasn't, Kate was almost sure, the same girl whose photo she had seen in Alexander's wallet. It was none of her business, she knew, whom he kissed, or whose picture he kept close to his heart—nor, for that matter, how many girlfriends he had, but all the same that tender greeting was puzzling, and, she realised with alarm, more upsetting than she wanted to admit after so brief an acquaintance.

Depressed, Kate watched the pair covertly. Alexander's arm was resting possessively round the dark girl's shoulders as he looked round, probably for her, but Kate kept her head down and slipped through the door and out into the sunshine to find the hire car that was supposed to be waiting for her.

She had no wish to play gooseberry or to be a witness to the loving intimacy the couple so clearly shared. It would be too painful. Far better to pretend to herself she'd never seen them and drive away now, before they also came out into the car park.

Miraculously she found her car where it was supposed to be, and in a short time Kate was driving along the dusty road towards the town of Kalamata en route for the Mani peninsula to the south and her home for the next two weeks.

She did her best not to feel too disappointed by this part of the journey. After all, the industrial outskirts of any town were seldom noted for their architectural beauty, and Liz had warned her that Kalamata, largely destroyed by an earthquake some years before, was still in the process of being rebuilt.

'Just wait till you see the house, though,' her friend had told her. 'That'll make up for anything, and the setting...it's just fantastic.'

It'd better be, Kate thought morosely as, having successfully negotiated the streets through the town, not long afterwards she found herself driving above a precipitous gorge along a road dotted with shrines whose purpose was all too clear.

Her spirits began to rise, though, as the road began to take a less alarming course through olive groves and the narrow streets of stone-built villages, hugging the coastline so that the sea was an almost constant companion as she continued southwards.

Mountains rose on one side of her, bare and uninhabited save for the occasional whitewashed church perched high on a summit, and on the other the ground sloped away through rock-strewn fields to the waters of the Mediterranean, brilliantly blue beneath the late spring sun and tempting Kate to stop to feast her eyes on the view.

Later, she promised herself. Now she must get on. There'd be plenty of time for exploring over the next two weeks, and suddenly, as she stepped on the accelerator, a feeling of impatient expectancy swept over her at the prospect of having all that time to indulge herself. She could go where she liked, eat when it suited her— or not at all, if she wasn't hungry. She could sleep in, stay up all night, and do exactly what she, Kate Penwarden, pleased, for almost the first time in her life, she realised with a shock.

Even Michael seemed a remote and not very important figure, and as for the business, apart from making one or two telephone calls to check that everything was ticking over, she'd put the whole enterprise out of her mind. She was here to enjoy herself, and enjoy herself she would.

The house, when she found it at last, came up to all her expectations and was every bit as attractive as Liz had described it.

Like most of the other houses in the region it was constructed of the local grey stone, standing alone at the end of a track leading away from the sea through yet another olive grove just at the foot of the mountains which formed the backbone of the peninsula.

There was, she knew, a village on the other side of the main road, handy enough for her daily needs, but tucked out of sight beneath the slope of the land, and when she got out of the car and gazed around there was not another building in sight.

All around were trees and wild shrubs, some now in flower, and in the distance, just visible through the branches, was the sea, still blue and sparkling.

Kate felt all the vestiges of the tension she had brought with her slip from her shoulders like a shabby coat, and she stretched up her arms to the sun in an almost pagan gesture of gratitude.

'What a place,' she murmured. 'What a lovely, perfect place.'

She stood there for a few minutes breathing in the clear, crisp air, unwilling to move and disturb the tranquillity she felt settling round her; then, with a little sigh of regret, she turned her back on the view and let herself into the house, staring round with delight.

It wasn't big, but whoever had converted it from the old farm building it had originally been had certainly had more than their fair share of imagination, for by clever use of space and light it gave an impression of being much larger than it really was, almost open-plan with a large living-room taking up most of the ground floor and a neat, well-equipped kitchen partially divided from it by an archway.

The walls were white and bright rugs on the marble floor provided splashes of colour here and there. The furniture had also been chosen carefully with an eye for design as well as comfort.

Upstairs there were two small double bedrooms, just as attractively furnished, and a practical bathroom. All that anyone could want for two idyllic weeks' holiday, Kate decided happily as she began to unpack her bags, thanking her lucky stars—or the Fates—that Liz happened to have a friend married to a Greek who had bought this cottage to have a base in his native country.

Also, that they hadn't wanted it themselves at this particular moment.

Kate's eye fell on the folder containing the publicity material she had brought with her to study, the papers she had dropped centuries ago in the airport cafeteria, and which Alexander...

She sighed. Why had those same Fates so unkindly brought them together just now, of all times, when she had decided not to have anything further to do with men—any man? And then, when she had been lulled into a false sense of security by his easy charm and generosity, to find he was already attached...it wasn't fair, it simply wasn't fair, she told herself as she shoved the folder back into her suitcase. Time enough to peruse it when she'd settled in—although she really ought to ring Liz and find out if Peter was getting on with the graphics, just to put her mind at rest and give herself something else to think about—not to mention banishing a certain pair of grey eyes from her memory.

Maybe now would be as good a time as any. So, where was the telephone?

It didn't take Kate long to discover there wasn't one, and, although she told herself firmly that she had come here to relax and that she could ring tomorrow from the village, she couldn't help feeling uneasy. She'd never been absolutely out of touch with her business before. What if something went wrong? How would Liz be able to reach her?

It even went through her mind that perhaps Liz had suggested her coming here just so that she couldn't be reached, before she told herself firmly to stop being paranoid. Of course nothing would go wrong. She must forget all about work, and enjoy herself. The sun was shining; what was she waiting for?

By the time Kate went up to bed that evening at an hour she would have considered ridiculously early back home in London, she had quite fallen in love with the little village down by the sea with its small harbour and simple taverns, in one of which she had treated herself to a late lunch. There was a supermarket, and you could buy fish straight from the boats, she'd been told, if you were there early enough.

Tomorrow, she told herself dreamily as she closed her eyes. Tomorrow she would take a walk along the cliff-top to the next village where, she had discovered from one of the guide-books on a shelf downstairs, there was a Byzantine church with marvellous frescoes. Or she could take the car and go further afield, visit Areopolis, perhaps ... after she had telephoned Liz, of course ...

The following morning, however, all Kate really felt like doing was curling up in a chair, or even on her bed, with the lightest and most undemanding book she could find.

She couldn't be bothered to go down to the village for fresh bread for breakfast, although the night before she had resolved to have an early walk each day, picking up a loaf from the baker's on the way home. Instead, she wandered lethargically about the house, only just able to summon up the energy to brew a pot of coffee, and when it was made she flopped on to a chair with a cup, thankful she wasn't obliged to make any further effort.

'This is ridiculous,' she told herself out loud when half the morning had slipped by without her even having noticed it. 'Here you are, Kate Penwarden, in this beautiful spot with the whole of Greece outside your front door waiting to be explored, and all you can do is lounge about, not even properly dressed, wishing you were back in bed. Come on, stir yourself.'

Kate grinned sheepishly as she got to her feet. Talking to herself now, was she? The first sign of madness that was supposed to be, and she couldn't go mad, not yet, and certainly not here. She shook her head, then closed her eyes briefly as a sharp pain stabbed through it. What was the matter with her? Even her legs felt leaden as she forced them up the stairs.

She must be suffering from the delayed effects of the journey coming on top of the strains she'd been under at work—not to mention other, more personal troubles. She must have been more stressed than she'd thought.

She dressed slowly, and decided to take the car for a drive down the coast. Her walk could be postponed for another day, and she didn't really feel she would appreciate the frescoes, not today, with her head feeling so woolly.

In her own car and on a road she knew well, one which didn't corkscrew round itself as it climbed the side of the mountain in a series of hairpin bends, Kate would have reached her planned destination with no trouble at all, but as it was the muzziness in her head seemed to increase with each gear-wrenching turn, and a glance down to the sea at the foot of the cliffs she was climbing so steeply just made her feel giddy, and again there was that stab of pain behind her eyes, making her blink and swerve dangerously close to the unprotected edge of the road.

This won't do, she told herself as she tried to gather up her straying concentration. I must find somewhere to turn and go home before someone has to put another shrine on this stretch of road.

Just ahead there was a sort of lay-by, strewn with litter and boulders, but just wide enough for her to be able to turn the car round, she thought. Kate drove up to it, put the car into reverse and her foot down, then there was a sickening jolt that threw her forward, and the world went black.

Some time later, and she had no idea how much later, Kate became vaguely aware of gentle hands touching her, strong arms lifting her carefully and laying her down with something soft beneath her head, and of a deep voice that seemed strangely familiar murmuring comforting words to her.

Then she appeared to be moving, swerving, swaying...and she lost consciousness again, accepting oblivion gratefully as it eased the painful throbbing in her head.

When at last she did cautiously open her eyes some time later Kate was astonished to find herself lying in a bed in a totally unfamiliar room darkened by drawn curtains so that she was unable to see every detail of her surroundings.

There was enough light, however, to tell her that she wasn't alone. In the far corner, reading by a shaded lamp, was the figure of a girl. A nurse, could she be? Was she in hospital, then, she wondered vaguely. This room certainly didn't look like a ward, not if the homely furnishings were anything to go by. So where...?

Kate tried to struggle into a sitting position, but at the first sign of movement the girl in the corner was on her feet.

'No, no,' she said in a soft, attractively accented voice. 'You must not move. Tell me what you want and I can get it for you.'

Firm yet gentle hands pressed Kate back into the pillows where she subsided with a sigh, frowning as she looked up into the smiling face bending over her—a face she had seen somewhere before, surely?

Then it all came back to her. This was the girl Alexander had met off the plane from Athens, whom he had kissed so affectionately. So whose house was this?

'Where am I?' Kate asked worriedly. 'And how did I get here?'

'Don't you remember? Alexander found you—you'd had an accident in the car. Nothing too serious, but you'd knocked yourself out.'

Kate put her hands to her head feeling utterly confused. 'No, I can't remember anything.'

'It doesn't matter,' the girl reassured her with a gentle smile. 'It will all come back when you've rested.'

'And this is Alexander's house?' Kate persisted.

'That's right—well, his and mine, I suppose,' she added cheerily, unconscious of the effect her words were having on Kate's spirits. 'But don't concern yourself with any of that. Maybe you'd like a drink? The doctor said it would be all right.'

'The doctor?' Kate echoed in some alarm. 'Surely I haven't been examined by a doctor. I can't have been that unconscious.'

The girl Kate now knew to be Alexander's wife was quick to reassure her. 'No, not yet. He'll come later, just to check we're looking after you properly,' she smiled. 'Alexander rang him up to tell him what had happened. You were lucky he came across you so quickly. What were——? No,' she shook her head. 'We'll leave explanations till later. Just rest now.'

She slipped an arm behind Kate's head and supported her while she took a sip of water, then rearranged the pillows as Kate sank back again with a grimace of pain.

'My head,' she groaned. 'It feels as though a hammer's hit it.'

'Not a hammer,' Alexander's wife informed her. 'Just the steering-wheel. You hit it when the car ran into the rock.'

'The rock?' Kate couldn't remember any rock, but suddenly it didn't seem to matter. She closed her eyes and floated off again into a state of semi-wakefulness in which people's voices, a man's and a woman's, murmured a comforting background to her drifting thoughts.

Later on the doctor called, a round, twinkling man who couldn't speak a word of English but who, according to Alexander's wife, who was acting as interpreter, pronounced himself satisfied that there was no damage done, only a case of mild concussion on top of the viral infection Kate had already been suffering from when she'd woken that morning.

'And now all you need is rest.'

Kate's eyes flicked over to the doorway where Alexander was standing, holding a tray. 'May I come in?'

Kate's first instinct was to try to tidy her dishevelled hair, knowing what a mess she must look, but at a time like this vanity had no place. She smiled weakly across at him. 'Yes, of course.'

She eased herself up in the bed, pulling the sheet firmly round her as Alexander crossed the room towards her. He brought a table over to the bed and placed the tray carefully on it.

'Just some soup,' he said. 'Light and nourishing fare for an invalid.'

The grey eyes met hers, their amused gleam softened now by an expression of concern she hadn't noticed before, and to her annoyance she felt an unwanted tremor flutter in her stomach. Hunger, she told herself crossly even as she smiled back at him. He's only being kind, and he belongs to someone else.

'I'm not an invalid,' she asserted, 'just someone stupid enough to...' She frowned and shook her head, then winced at the ache this movement produced. 'Actually, I don't know what did happen,' she confessed. 'I remember not feeling very well, and thinking I ought to go home, then——' She broke off, her eyes wide with perplexity.

'It doesn't matter now,' Alexander said firmly. 'Just eat your supper before it goes cold, and we can go into all the whys and wherefores when you're feeling stronger. There's no need to worry about anything.'

'But my car——' Kate began.

'That's all been taken care of,' Alexander assured her. 'I've rung the local garage and someone'll go and collect it and put right anything that needs to be done. You can have it back when you're fit to drive, and in the meantime you're staying here with us. No argument.'

He smiled down at her then turned to leave her to eat her meal in peace.

Kate hadn't realised she was hungry, but one mouthful of the delicious chicken broth told her otherwise, and by the time Alexander's wife came to collect her tray everything on it had been finished up.

'That's good,' she smiled. 'And you look better too, not so feverish. I expect you'd like to wash. If you feel strong enough, I'll show you where the bathroom is. Here, put this wrap round you.'

'It's so kind of you to look after me like this. You've even lent me a nightie,' Kate said gratefully, looking down at the unfamiliar garment as the other girl placed a supporting hand under her elbow. 'I hope Alexander doesn't make a habit of bringing stray females home to be cared for.'

'Oh, I do it all the time,' a cheerful voice called up from the bottom of the staircase. 'It's quite a hobby of mine, rescuing damsels in distress. I thought you'd have realised that by now.'

Feeling a lot more human and presentable after a wash and tidy up Kate came out of the bathroom to find Alexander hovering nearby to help her back to her room.

'Unless you'd rather come downstairs?' he enquired solicitously.

To her disgust Kate's legs gave a warning wobble and she shook her head as he took her arm.

'Perhaps later on,' she told him with an apologetic smile. 'I still feel a bit shaky, actually.'

She climbed gratefully back into bed and looked up at Alexander, her face serious. 'Honestly, I feel so embarrassed. It was all my fault. I should never have gone out in the car at all when I was feeling so peculiar, but I thought it was just the effect of the journey and——'
She paused, thinking how feeble that sounded, yet unwilling to go into further explanations to this man who was still only a stranger, after all.

'And?' Alexander prompted, then, sensing Kate's unease, he smiled reassuringly. 'There's no need to be embarrassed. I'm just glad I was around so soon after the accident happened.'

Kate lay back with a sigh. 'So am I, but I'm sorry I'm putting you and your wife to all this trouble. I'm sure I'll be able——'

Again she broke off in mid-sentence, but this time it was the expression on Alexander's face that brought her to a halt. His eyebrows shot up and his jaw dropped open in astonished amusement as he gave a roar of laughter.

'My *wife*? You thought Maria was my wife?'

Taken aback, Kate said rather stiffly, 'Well, no one's ever told me she isn't. Isn't she, then?' she added slowly, the implications of his reaction suddenly penetrating her still rather muddled brain and increasing the rate of her heartbeat as she waited for his answer.

'She's my sister,' Alexander told her, his eyes dancing. 'Neither of us, much to our parents' chagrin, is married, not at the moment.'

If, as he finished speaking, a sudden bleakness clouded his normally open features, Kate was in no fit state to notice. She fell back on to the pillows, forgetting momentarily all her fine protestations to herself about eliminating men from her life, and the last thought that went through her mind before she drifted off into a contented doze was that Alexander Dimitrakos wasn't, after all, a married man.

CHAPTER THREE

KATE lay back on her pillows listening with half an ear to the muted conversation downstairs and the unfamiliar sounds outside the window, trying not to feel too elated by her unexpected discovery of Alexander's bachelor status.

After all, he had said neither he nor Maria was married 'at the moment', and that might mean anything. What about that photo tucked into his wallet? They could well both be engaged, and she knew that betrothals in Greece were serious affairs that involved family honour to a much greater extent than was the case back home.

Anyway, why should it matter so much to her? She must not let herself be carried away by a pair of merry grey eyes or by Alexander's undoubted charm and sympathy, and, she reminded herself firmly, she should be especially on her guard just now when her resistance was at a particularly low ebb. Men, she had already decided, were to have no part in her future. The sooner she left this hospitable home, the better.

But it was not to be that easy.

'Of course you won't be leaving tomorrow,' Maria protested later that evening when she and her brother had come to see if Kate had everything she needed for the night. 'Apart from the bump on your head, you've got that virus, don't forget. You'll have to stay with us for at least another day—probably two.'

'And you can't escape, can you?' Alexander pointed out with inescapable logic. 'You haven't got a car, and I don't suppose you have any idea where you are.'

Kate gazed helplessly up at them. 'I don't know why you're being so kind to me. You don't know me at all, after all. I'm a perfect stranger to both of you.'

'Not quite true,' Alexander murmured, then drew himself up to fix her with an almost steely gaze. 'In Greece we have a tradition of offering help to strangers—perfect or otherwise. It's called *philoxenia* and it goes back to the beginning of time itself. You would insult us by leaving before you are quite fit—and besides,' he added in a softly teasing tone as Maria turned to leave the room, 'it's a pleasure to see you can accept help when you're unable to use your prickles.'

He reached out and touched her cheek gently, then withdrew his hand before his sister noticed and before Kate had time to react as their eyes met and held for a brief moment. Then he too turned to leave her.

'Goodnight, Kate,' he said in his normal voice, 'and sleep well.'

The sun was high in the sky and shafting through the gap in the curtains when Kate awoke the following day.

For a moment she couldn't remember where she was, then it all came back to her and she stretched her limbs tentatively down to the end of the bed, sensing with relief that the strength had returned to them. She put a hand to her head, which no longer felt hot and dry as it had done the day before, though there was still a painful bruise on her forehead where she had cracked it against the steering-wheel.

She wriggled into a sitting position and reached for her watch. Eleven o'clock? It couldn't be, could it?

She swung her legs over the side of the bed and walked—quite steadily, she was glad to note—to the window and peered out. As Alexander had observed the day before, she had no idea where she was, but what she saw now made her eyes sparkle with delight, for the house was right down on the water's edge fronting a quayside on the edge of a wide bay, the sea only a few metres from the front door.

She flung the window open and leant out to take in great lungfuls of the clear, salty air, quite oblivious of the fact that she still only had on Maria's thin cotton nightdress, which revealed rather more of her curves than she might have chosen to do in these circumstances.

'So you're feeling better? Why don't you come down? It's beautiful out here—and the view is spectacular!'

Kate hadn't noticed that Alexander was one of a group of men chatting by a fishing-boat that had obviously just come in, to judge by the boxes of fish they were unloading. He gazed admiringly up at her, making her suddenly aware of her semi-clothed state, and she withdrew quickly, her cheeks colouring.

She pulled on her clothes, a short-sleeved shirt and jeans, washed her face and gave her hair a quick brush, then ran downstairs, slowing to a more sedate pace as she went outside to join Alexander.

His eyes ran appraisingly over her now decently covered body.

'Pity,' he murmured, his mouth twitching with amusement at the glare Kate gave him, then he tucked her arm proprietorially into his and led her over to the spot where he'd been standing earlier.

'How d'you fancy one of these for dinner this evening?'

Kate peered at the strange assortment of fish, nothing like those she was used to seeing back home in her local supermarket.

'I think you'd better choose,' she said doubtfully. 'They all look equally unfamiliar to me.'

Alexander laughed and released her arm to squat down beside the boat, and Kate felt something knot in the pit of her stomach as she noted, less objectively than she would have wished, the taut curves of his thigh muscles moulded by the denim of his jeans, and the straight lines of his broad back...

She turned away quickly and strolled along the quayside while Alexander finished haggling with the boatmen, and by the time he caught up with her she had more or less regained her equanimity and come to a decision.

'I can't go on imposing on you and Maria,' she told him. 'I honestly feel a lot better today, and if you could take me home—when it's convenient, of course—I'll be fine.'

'Out of the question,' Alexander returned firmly. 'Not today, anyway. You may *feel* better, and I'm very glad you do, but the doctor was quite firm that you needed several days' rest. After all, you were concussed, remember, and you need an eye kept on you until the effects have worn off completely. Besides,' he added, opening his plastic carrier to show her the contents, 'Maria and I can't possibly eat all these ourselves. You've got to stay and share them with us.'

Kate allowed a resigned sigh to escape her and Alexander's mouth curved into a wry smile.

'Aren't you happy here with us, Kate? I'm sorry if you don't feel welcome.'

'No, of course I'm happy,' she was quick to assure him, 'and I don't know when I've been made to feel so welcome. It's just——' She paused, frowning.

'Yes?' Alexander prompted her.

Kate gave a rueful shrug. 'I suppose I'm not used to being taken care of. I've always managed well enough on my own till now, and it's an unfamiliar experience to be told what I must or mustn't do.'

'Your prickles are showing again,' Alexander remarked drily, 'and of course if you really want to leave us and be on your own there's nothing we can do to prevent you. You're not a hostage or anything. I just thought you needed help, but perhaps I was wrong.'

He turned and walked swiftly away back towards the house, leaving Kate staring uncertainly after him. Had she really hurt him, personally, or was it the Greek—what was it? *Philoxenia*, hospitality?—that had been offended by her apparent lack of gratitude?

She hurried after him, only catching him up outside his house as he stopped to open the door.

'Alexander, I'm sorry. I didn't mean to offend you,' she said, raising wide eyes to his. 'Of course I'm very grateful for all you and Maria have done for me. But I don't want to be a nuisance.'

To her dismay she felt her legs suddenly threaten to give way, and she swayed, clutching on to the doorframe for support.

Alexander dropped his bag of fish and caught her by the shoulders as a cloud swam across her vision, momentarily blotting out the brightness of the sky.

'I'm sorry,' she said helplessly, and put a hand to her head. 'I don't know what came over me.'

'I told you you weren't strong enough to go home. Perhaps now you'll believe me,' Alexander said firmly, half carrying her into the living-room where he placed her gently in a chair. 'You simply aren't fit to be on your own, are you? Admit it for once.'

Kate leant back and gazed up into his face. 'No, Alexander,' she said meekly. 'Maybe I'm not.'

To her horror tears of weakness welled up in her eyes and she blinked them back fiercely, but not before Alexander had seen them and reached out to wipe them away with one careful finger.

'You stay where you are and I'll fetch you something to drink. Orange juice?'

Kate nodded and closed her eyes as she listened to the comfortable sounds of Alexander moving about in the kitchen. Maybe she could, in spite of all her brave protestations of independence, get used to being cared for, after all. But Michael had wanted to do that, in his way, hadn't he? Or she'd thought he had, until her discovery that he had gone off with Carol, 'caring' for her so deeply that he'd given her a baby.

Waves of bitterness, shocking in their intensity, swept over her as she remembered again that dreadful, final meeting, and his wounding accusations, and it was only with a heroic effort of will that she managed to banish most, if not all, of these painful memories to the farthest recesses of her mind before Alexander came back into the room bearing a tray which he set down on a table by the side of Kate's chair.

'How does this look? I thought you might be hungry. After all, you can hardly have eaten anything yesterday.'

'It looks absolutely delicious,' Kate said enthusiastically as her eyes fell on the fresh bread, orange juice and dish of yogurt with a jar of honey beside it, all attractively laid out on a yellow cloth. 'You certainly know how to tempt a girl.'

There was a glint in the grey eyes that met hers and Alexander's wide mouth twitched.

'You could have fooled me,' he observed, 'but I'm glad my professional skills have succeeded where my charm has clearly failed.'

Kate felt the colour creep into her cheeks and bent her head quickly, taking a piece of bread and buttering it to hide the confusion she knew must be only too visible on her face.

'Professional skills?' she queried. 'You're not a waiter, surely?'

'I have been, in my time,' Alexander replied cheerfully, strolling over to the window where he leant back against the wall to study her with approval as she tucked into her breakfast. 'Barman, too, and chef—you name it, and I'll have done it.'

'You're in the restaurant business, then, as well as hotels?' Kate's hand paused midway to her lips as she took in this new perception of her host.

'I was. My father has a couple of restaurants in Scotland.'

'Scotland? Good heavens, how extraordinary!'

'How so?' Alexander returned interestedly. 'What's so extraordinary about Scotland? People do live there, and eat as well, I'm glad to say.'

'Yes, I know.' Kate sipped her orange juice thoughtfully. 'But it's an awful long way from here, and I thought this was your family home. Maybe I was wrong, though.'

'No, you're right on all counts, Miss Penwarden.'

Alexander came back to perch on the arm of the chair opposite her as he went on, 'My father left here and went to London when he was barely out of his teens. It was quite common then for young men to go abroad to earn money to send home. There's not much work round here, except in fishing—oh, and olives, of course—but not nearly enough to keep large families going. So off my dad went to London.'

'And then?' Kate prompted him, intrigued.

'And then, while he was working in a hôtel, he met the girl who was to become his wife and my mother— a Scots lass called Morag. She had an uncle with a restaurant, only a small affair, more of a café, really, in Glasgow, and when he became ill the two of them went up to run it for him. And it all developed from there. He—my father—now owns two restaurants and a hotel, and that's where I, and my brothers and sisters, too, learnt our trade. Our original trade, that is.'

And where you got your grey eyes from, Kate said silently. That was one mystery solved.

'But you're not still working for him?' she asked, stirring honey into the thick, creamy yogurt, then licking the spoon with childish glee. 'But the way, this is the most delicious breakfast I've had for ages—years, probably,' she told him with a grin. 'Even better than croissants in Paris.'

As soon as she had spoken Kate wished she hadn't made that last remark, for it brought back memories she'd have preferred to have left undisturbed, especially here, and now.

A slight frown creased her forehead as she spooned up the yogurt, and Alexander was quick to note her change of mood.

'Something wrong? Paris isn't a place usually associated with sadness,' he added lightly.

'I...I'd rather not talk about it,' Kate replied in a low voice. 'It's all over and done with now.'

There was a short silence, then, to change a subject she sensed was still hovering unresolved between them she asked, 'Where's Maria this morning?'

Alexander smiled. 'Meeting her fiancé, Manolis. He was driving down from Athens and she's gone to his parents' home to wait for him. That's the chief reason why she's here at the moment, and that's why I was meeting her at the airport—and, speaking of Manolis, that's just reminded me...' He glanced at the gold watch encircling his wrist, and got to his feet.

'Will you be all right if I go out for a while? I have to see him myself on a business matter, though if you don't feel well enough to be left...?'

'No, no, I'm fine,' Kate assured him hastily. 'You mustn't alter any arrangements because of me. Oh, and talking of business matters——' She paused, wondering whether she could broach the subject that had bothered her when she had been settling into her cottage, or whether it would be too much of an imposition.

'Well?' Alexander enquired. 'Go on, it's not like you to haver.'

'"Haver" isn't a word you'd expect to hear in this country.' She grinned, then bit her lip doubtfully. 'I was just wondering if I might use your phone to ring England—I'll leave you the money, of course,' she added quickly, 'but if I could ring my partner it would put my mind at rest that everything's in order back home. We're just going to open a second boutique, you see——'

'And yet you've come away on holiday?' Alexander sounded astonished, as well he might, Kate admitted privately as she raised bleak eyes to his, willing him not to pursue the subject. Some time, if the right occasion arose, she might tell him just why she had taken this trip, but not just at this moment.

To her relief Alexander merely gave a slight shrug as though dismissing the matter as none of his business, and then nodded. 'Of course—the phone's through there, in the kitchen. And I hope you find everything running smoothly. But don't overdo things, will you? Rest is what you need.'

'I won't,' she promised. 'As soon as I've spoken to Liz I'll go for a stroll, then I'll probably spend the rest of the day just sitting in the sun. After all, holidays are for being lazy, aren't they?' she ended in rather too bright a tone that caused Alexander's eyebrows to rise, unnoticed, but he said nothing. Maybe later he'd get a chance to find out the reason for that shadow behind the clear green eyes, but this was clearly neither the place, nor the time.

Kate duly made her telephone call to a surprised Liz, who reassured her in rather hurt tones that of course she had everything under control, and that Peter had promised his finished designs for later in the week.

'And stop worrying,' she said. 'For goodness' sake, Kate, you're supposed to be on holiday. Put all this behind you, just for a week or so. If there's a crisis I'll get in touch, but there won't be, so just enjoy yourself.'

Suppressing the uncomfortable realisation that there was no way Liz could easily get in touch without a phone in the cottage, Kate put the phone down and wandered back into the living-room to see if she could find a book to read to help pass the time until either Alexander or Maria returned, something light and not too de-

manding, she thought, browsing along the shelves, something——

'Oh!'

At the end of the row of books was a collection of
photographs, family groups mainly, and one of a proud
and happy Maria arm-linked with a smiling, dark-haired
man, presumably Manolis, but tucked in behind, almost
invisible from the front, was another photograph of
another pretty girl, the same one, Kate was almost sure,
whose picture Alexander carried in his wallet.

Kate picked it up to study it more closely. There was
no clue as to who it might be, no name or date even on
the back, and she stared at the calm, sweet face gazing
out of the frame, willing the mystery girl to give up her
secret.

Was Alexander engaged too, then, to this nameless
girl? He had never mentioned her, but then why should
he? Kate reflected gloomily. Theirs was only a passing
acquaintanceship, after all. There was no reason why he
should tell her anything about himself or his
relationships.

She weighed the photograph in her hand, then replaced it exactly where she had found it, wondering as
she did so why, if this was Alexander's fiancée, or girl-
friend, he didn't want her picture in a more prominent
position where he could see it and be reminded of her.

It was all very puzzling.

Her eyes then fell on another photo, a large family
group, this time, with an older couple, presumably Mr
and Mrs Dimitrakos, surrounded by adults and children
of all ages. She searched for Alexander and found him
standing just behind his father, laughing up at the small
boy perched high on his shoulder—his youngest brother,
maybe, or a nephew.

Then, as Kate looked from one member to another
of this happy, smiling group, a surge of envy and longing
swept through her so savage that it made her hand

tremble as she put the photograph back on the shelf, knowing these people shared something she had never known: the security that came from a close-knit, affectionate family.

She thought back to her own childhood, so different from that of the little boy in Alexander's arms, to her feckless mother and the father who had walked out on the two of them only days after she, Kate, had been born... and then remorselessly on to the series of ever more sordid bedsits she and her mother had called 'home' until the authorities had stepped in and sent her off to the first in a succession of foster homes.

And, knowing all this, Michael had wondered why she hadn't felt able to bring up a family of her own. How could she, with no maternal experience to fall back on? It wouldn't be fair on any child to have to rely on her as a mother.

Hastily, before she allowed herself to become totally immersed in a morass of self-pity, Kate turned away from the photograph and grabbed a book, a well-worn copy of a historical romance by Georgette Heyer, and took it out into the little garden behind the house where she read and dozed until her hosts returned later in the afternoon.

'This is shameful.' She grinned sheepishly at Maria. 'I don't know when I last did nothing at all for a whole day.'

'It will have been very good for you,' Maria asserted. 'Alexander tells me you run your own business, so I don't suppose you get much time to relax. And, after all, you did come here on holiday.'

'Even so...' Kate got up and stretched lazily. 'I can see myself spending the whole fortnight being totally idle if I don't make an effort to stir myself, and, talking of which, I simply can't go on imposing on you like this. I do feel much better now, and tomorrow I must leave you in peace and go back to my own place. Even if I have to walk. I've taken up quite enough of your time as it is.'

'There'll be no need for such drastic action,' Alexander laughed as he emerged from the back door. 'The garage is bringing your car back tomorrow, so if you do insist on leaving...?' Kate nodded vigorously. 'Well, I shall escort you back just to make sure you get there in one piece.'

'There's no need,' Kate began, then caught Alexander's determined eye. 'All right, I give in. Thanks very much,' she said with unaccustomed meekness.

'Your brother's very masterful, isn't he?' Kate sighed with mock resignation as she followed Maria into the kitchen. 'He's not very willing to take no for an answer.'

'Like most Greek men,' Maria laughed. 'But as long as you pretend to give in, you can usually twist them round your little finger.'

'So tell me about your fiancé,' Kate said as she watched the other girl deftly clean the fish Alexander had bought that morning. 'Does he live here, or in Athens? Have you known him long?'

While Maria worked she filled Kate in on some further details of their family history. Although she and Manolis had not met until they were in their teens there had been close ties between the two families even before the time Maria's and Alexander's father had left home for London.

'And that's not as usual as you think, in this part of Greece,' Maria told her. 'Feuds, quite bloody ones, are more common among neighbouring families than friendships, I can tell you.'

'And what does Manolis do for a living?' Kate asked interestedly.

'Hotel management. Has Alexander told you about his new venture?' Maria enquired, apparently changing the subject.

Kate shook her head. 'I don't even know what *his* line of business is either, except that he owns a hotel near Athens airport—oh, and that he's a very good waiter.'

Maria laughed. 'Even I couldn't tell you exactly what he does, and I'm not sure he knows himself. He has fingers in so many pies it's impossible to keep up with him.'

Alexander came in to join the two girls at that moment, blocking up the doorway as he leant his large frame against the wall.

'And the latest pie is a new hotel complex up on the headland behind us. Very exclusive, and very beautiful. You'll have to let me show you round some time.'

'And Manolis and I are going to run it,' Maria smiled happily, arranging the fish on the grill pan.

'And there's another thing you must experience while you're here—in the Mani, that is,' Alexander told Kate. He nodded at the fish. 'Those will be delicious, Maria will see to that, but there's only one way to appreciate these fish properly, and that's cooked on an open fire on a beach miles from anywhere—preferably with a beautiful girl as the sun is going down over the sea.' His eyebrow lifted lazily as he glanced sideways at Kate. 'We'll take my boat out one evening before you go home to England and you can see what I mean. It will be an experience you will never forget, I promise you.'

'I'm sure,' Kate murmured, suddenly tempted beyond belief by the prospect of such a romantic trip. Simultaneously alarmed at the reaction of her pulse-rate to the picture Alexander had conjured up in her mind, she turned away to make some casual remark to Maria, unaware of the gleam in the perceptive grey eyes that caught the quickening flush on her cheek.

The sooner she returned to her solitary and independent existence the better. Emotional entanglements of any kind, however transitory, were definitely not on her schedule.

* * *

But Kate had not reckoned on the possibility that she might actually feel lonely once she had settled back into the little stone cottage that was her temporary home.

'If there's anything you want, just ring us,' Alexander had told her as he was about to leave.

Good as his word, he had driven behind her all the way back, and waited to see her safely settled in before deciding she was quite capable of coping on her own.

'Or, better still, drop round. You know where our house is now, and it's not far. But no more accidents, mind. You might swerve the wrong way next time.'

Kate shuddered. 'And there might not be a knight errant riding by to rescue me,' she acknowledged lightly. She looked up at him, her wide, green eyes serious as she went on, 'I can't tell you how grateful I am to you and Maria for all you've done for me. Especially after...'

She broke off, but Alexander was quick to pick up her meaning. 'After trying to fend me off with your prickles,' he observed with a wry smile. 'I am pretty thick-skinned, though, and not so easily put off once I set my mind on something, like helping a damsel in distress against her will.'

'My will couldn't put up much resistance, as it turned out,' Kate admitted ruefully, 'and, as I said, I truly am grateful.'

She held out her hand and Alexander took it in both of his, pulling her nearer to him and bending swiftly to brush her lips with his—just the lightest of kisses, but one which left her staring after him as he strode away down the path to his waiting car with a grin over his shoulder and a wave of his hand.

'Bye, Kate. See you around, and take care.'

Then he wheeled the car round, sending up a cloud of dust behind him, and he was gone.

Kate had returned to the house more disconsolately than she cared to admit and found her fingers straying to her mouth, touching it lightly as his lips had done; a pang shot through her as she wondered what it would be like to feel them pressed more urgently to her own, his arms holding her against that broad chest...

No, an inner voice ordered her. You mustn't even think those things. He means nothing to you—and you can mean nothing whatever to him. Nothing! Do you hear? Remember that photograph.

'I hear,' Kate muttered to herself. 'But you don't have to go on about it. There's no harm in fantasising, especially as there's no chance of ever being in his—or any other man's—arms. It's the single, unattached life for me from now on.'

All these brave admonishments to herself didn't stop her missing the kindness and easy banter of the sister and brother who had so willingly befriended her, and her solitary midday meal at the village taverna somehow lost its appeal, especially when she looked round at the other tables occupied by locals and holiday-makers, families, couples and groups, all enjoying themselves and none of them sitting alone as she was.

It might be better to eat back in the cottage, Kate thought with a sigh as she paid the bill and strolled along the road fronting the beach. At least then she wouldn't have to put up with the sight of so many people enjoying themselves.

She sat on a seat beneath a dusty tree and stared out to sea. What was the matter with her? She had come here expressly to be alone, to relax without the pressure of having to consider anyone else's wishes, and, if anyone was used to fending for herself, she was. How else could she have built up her business into the success it was now? Liz, after all, had only come on the scene when business was already booming.

The bump on her head must have affected her more than she had realised, and the best thing to do for a fit of the blues was to find something positive to do—like go round the little supermarket and find something to cook for supper, for instance.

Hadn't there been a Greek recipe book back in the living-room? With a bit of improvisation and ingenuity she could probably experiment on a number of new dishes she could try out on her friends back home and, she thought with rising excitement, she could invite Alexander and Maria, and Manolis too, round for a meal in a day or two as a thank-you for their hospitality.

A dinner party would give her something to think about and plan for and, a different small voice whispered deep in her heart, give her a bona fide excuse for getting in touch with Alexander and seeing him again.

The rest of the day she spent happily planning the menu, and in the evening she went back to the village to ring the number of Alexander's house.

'Hello, Kate,' he said, obviously surprised at hearing her so soon. 'Nothing's wrong, is it? Are you in need of a knight to rescue you again?'

A tremor of some emotion she couldn't—or didn't want to—identify flickered through Kate at the sound of the deep, attractively accented voice, and she could see the dancing light of gently teasing mockery in his eyes as clearly as though he were there beside her.

'Kate, are you there? *Is* something the matter? You're not feeling ill again, are you?'

His bantering tone had changed to one of real concern and brought her quickly back to earth.

'No, nothing like that. Sorry—I was just thinking about something...' Her voice trailed off as she chided herself again for her susceptibility. 'No,' she repeated more firmly, 'I was just ringing to ask you if you and Maria, and Manolis, of course, if he'd like to, would come over for a meal one evening. Just as a way of saying thank you for your hospitality—your *philoxenia*,' she added with a little laugh.

'That's very kind, but there's no need, especially as you are supposed to be on holiday.'

'I'd like to,' Kate insisted. 'It'll give me something to think about. I'm not used to a life of complete idleness — and it will stop me brooding about work.'

She heard Alexander chuckle. 'In that case, we should obviously be doing you a favour!'

There was a short pause and the sound of muffled voices. 'Maria says to say we accept with pleasure, purely as therapy, you understand, and would the day after tomorrow suit you?'

'That would be fine,' Kate told him, trying not to sound too eager. 'I'll look forward to seeing you all then.'

Over the next couple of days Kate found herself anticipating the dinner party with an excitement quite out of proportion to the event, and more than once she was assailed by waves of doubt over the wisdom of the enterprise.

She knew herself too well to delude herself that it was merely the prospect of a party, and a small one at that, that made her heart dance each time she thought of it, so why tempt Fate by inviting complications, in the shape of Alexander, a man whom she barely knew, into her house—and her life, which she had come here to sort out?

Hadn't she kept telling herself, over and over again, after the traumatic break-up with Michael, that men were to be kept strictly at arm's length from now on? So why go back so feebly on her resolve to keep herself to herself?

But inviting Alexander to a meal could hardly be called involvement, she reasoned, as she gazed out at the olive orchard outside her kitchen window, and when it was over there was no reason or excuse why their paths should ever cross again. In any case, she wouldn't be alone with him. Maria and Manolis would be here, too, and what could be more natural than showing her gratitude to them all in this simple way?

But the Fates had their own idea on how they wanted to shape the pattern of events. On the day of the dinner party, and just as Kate was letting herself into the cottage laden with all the vegetables she needed for the meal she heard the sound of a car driving up the track.

'Alexander!' she breathed, her heart pumping uncomfortably as she watched him climb out and come across to her.

'Don't worry,' he called out, 'there's nothing wrong,— or nothing serious, anyway—and we haven't all gone mad and arrived early.'

'But you can't come.' Kate heard herself sounding as flat as she felt.

'Not exactly. Here, let's go in, you'll be dropping those if you go on standing there.'

They went through to the kitchen where Kate deposited her load on the table while Alexander explained that Maria had woken up with one of the migraines that laid her low from time to time.

'There's nothing she can do but stay in bed till it passes—usually at least a day, and Manolis——'

'Won't want to come without her. I can see that. Poor Maria, I am sorry, but tell her not to worry. We can easily fix another day.'

'But you've already bought everything, haven't you? And got the preparations under way, too, I expect?'

'Well——' Kate hedged, unwilling to tell him a direct lie. 'I have made a start. Look——' her cheeks went slightly pink as she went on rather too quickly '—you couldn't come anyway, I suppose? You can see I've got rather a lot for just one...' She gestured towards the vegetables heaped up between them. 'And most of it won't keep.'

'That would be very nice,' Alexander said gravely though with the suspicion of a smile at the corners of his mouth. 'I shall be honoured to accept your invitation, and I shall look forward to the evening very much.'

Not as much as I shall, Kate thought with a surge of guilty elation as she heard him sweep off down the track. She never gave a thought to the fact that it was only a few days ago that she was doing her best to keep at arm's length the irritating man who would insist on chattering to her. As for all those brave resolutions about avoiding the company of men ... they were pushed firmly to the deepest recesses of her mind—for this one day, at least.

'My goodness!' Alexander exclaimed, following these words with something incomprehensible—Greek, Kate assumed—that clearly meant the same thing.

He stood in the doorway, towering over her, the eyes that appraised her appearance wide with unfeigned admiration and surprise, too, and Kate found herself blushing like a schoolgirl.

'I should cultivate my habit of rescuing damsels in distress,' he murmured as he took her hand and raised it to his lips, 'if this is going to be the result.'

Kate looked down at the flimsy material of her skirt, all swirling bronze and copper—colours that complemented the shining chestnut of her hair—and glad that she had chosen, after agonies of indecision, this particular dress for the occasion. Not that that there had been a great deal of choice. She hadn't come away with any idea of socialising, and had packed this dress on a last-minute impulse, 'just in case', she had told herself, though just in case of what she could hardly have imagined then.

'Thank you for the compliment, *kyrie*.' She curtsyed pertly, and turned quickly to lead the way inside hoping to hide the racing pulses in her neck, not to mention the only too obvious brightness in her eye at the sight of him standing there before her, so tall and, she realised for almost the first time since they had met, so over-poweringly masculine.

Again, and far too late, she wondered just how wise she had been in inviting Alexander here on his own.

CHAPTER FOUR

THERE was a little patio at the back of the house with a couple of chairs and a table set among the multitude of containers that later in the year would be an overflowing mass of colour. Even now a rose and a few early geraniums made the place look bright and welcoming, and Alexander settled himself in a chair and looked about him with interest.

'This is very pleasant. Who did you say the house belongs to?'

'A friend of a friend—Yannis Pavlides, his name is, and he's married to an English girl, Penny, who's a good friend of my best friend and business partner, Liz—if you follow me?'

'Just about,' Alexander grinned. 'Liz is the lady you rang the other day, I seem to remember. I never asked, is everything running smoothly back home in your absence? As well as the plans for your second boutique, of course.'

He leant back and stretched his long legs out in front of him, watching Kate as she brought out a tray of drinks from the house.

'You have a good memory,' she told him, surprised.

'Like a computer,' Alexander agreed, 'where business matters are concerned.'

He sipped his drink, eyeing her thoughtfully over the edge of his glass which he turned lazily in long fingers. 'So tell me about the boutiques. What do you sell, and who to?'

'Well . . .' Kate frowned. She hadn't expected this kind of conversation, but still, if he was really interested . . .

'We aim at the kind of young businesswomen who want well-designed clothes and don't mind spending a little more than average on looking good,' she told him. 'We get quite a lot of our things from a young French designer—Nicole Latour. It was her idea to expand, and the new shop's going to be in Brighton, and we hope to open in a couple of months.'

Alexander raised his eyebrows. 'But now you've come away on holiday?'

Kate was quick to catch his meaning and pulled a rueful face. 'Liz thought I needed a break, for one reason or another...' Her voice trailed off and she turned away to fiddle with the bottles on the table beside her.

'Paris?' Alexander suggested.

'Paris?' Kate's head shot up in surprise. 'What——?'

Alexander smiled gently. 'The same look came into your eyes the other day when you mentioned Paris, and I wondered... I'm sorry, I should have kept my mouth shut, shouldn't I? Tell me instead about the new boutique. Will you be aiming at a different market in Brighton? More of a leisure emphasis, maybe?'

With an effort Kate suppressed the image of Michael, wandering down the Champs Elysées with Carol smiling into his eyes, then sharing an intimate dinner in some romantic, no doubt very expensive restaurant before sauntering back to their hotel, to make love...

'Kate?'

'Oh—sorry.' She wrenched her mind back to her business and to Alexander's quite searching questions.

'Are you angling for a takeover?' she enquired lightly as they moved into the house a little later. 'You seem very curious about my affairs.'

She looked back at him over her shoulder and saw his eyes glint.

'A takeover,' he murmured. 'That's something I hadn't thought of. I wonder——'

'Wonder away, Mr Dimitrakos,' Kate said tartly. 'I haven't worked as hard as I have over the past few years to have my success stolen from me just when it's beginning to take off.'

'Fair enough,' Alexander acknowledged mildly, 'but all the same, the general idea's not a bad one. How about a partnership, instead? Dimitrakos and Penwarden—or the other way round, if you'd prefer,' he added hastily, pretending to flinch away at the light of battle flashing in Kate's eyes.

'I've already got one partner, and I think that's enough for now, thanks,' Kate told him firmly. 'But if I ever need another, I'll let you know.'

'I'll hold you to that.'

There was a new and challenging light in Alexander's eyes which threatened to do uncomfortable things to her heartbeat, and she turned hastily to lead the way into the living-room where the dining table was already set and waiting.

'Would you like to sit down?' she invited him. 'I don't know about you, but I'm starving.'

As she pulled a chair out for him his arm brushed against hers, making a tremor run along the nerve-ends, but with a valiant effort of will she forced herself to ignore this brief contact. She mustn't, she simply mustn't allow herself to fall victim to this man's undoubted charm and physical attraction.

During the meal Kate made sure the conversation kept to completely non-controversial topics, guiding it away from her own personal affairs whenever she felt Alexander might be tempted to probe a little too deeply into her reasons for taking this solitary holiday.

As she would have expected, he made an entertaining companion, telling her something of the turbulent history of this part of Greece and the colourful characters like Mavromichalis—Black Michael—who had led the revolt against the occupying Turks.

'There's a statue of him in Areopolis,' Alexander told her. 'You can't miss it if you go there—it's quite a landmark, bang in the middle of the square.'

'Black Michael,' Kate echoed faintly. 'I'll keep a look out for him.'

There was a moment's silence and Alexander looked across at Kate's bent head and nodded slowly to himself, but before he could speak Kate asked brightly, 'So what about some coffee? Unless you'd like another helping of the chicken—there's plenty left.'

'I've had more than enough, thanks.' Alexander leaned back in his chair and smiled across at Kate. 'It was a delicious meal. Maria and Manolis don't know what they've been missing, and I'm very glad you allowed me to come on my own—although...'

He paused long enough to drain the last of his wine then put his glass down thoughtfully, resting his elbows on the table as his eyes narrowed.

'I've just realised, Miss Penwarden, that I don't know much more about you than I did when I arrived here. Except that you are clearly a very successful and resourceful businesswoman, and also a very good cook. That fish soup was really excellent.'

Kate bowed her head in mock modesty. 'Thank you, sir, I'm glad you enjoyed it.'

She got up quickly to forestall any further remarks of a more personal nature and repeated her enquiry about the coffee.

'I know it's not customary here to finish off a meal with it, but I'd like a cup...unless you want yours Greek? That's something I'm afraid I haven't even attempted yet.'

'I could show you how. Let's see what there is in the kitchen.'

It was while Kate had her back to Alexander and was stretching to open one of the cupboards that she realised,

too late, that she had played right into his hands—
literally.

Before she could make even the feeblest attempt to
escape she felt his arms go round her waist, imprisoning
her against his chest. As she bent her head to push inef-
fectually at his strong hands she felt his soft breath on
the back of her neck then, a second later, the touch of
his lips caressing the skin just above the scooped neckline
of her dress.

'Alexander,' she protested, 'that's not——'

'Not what?' he breathed into her ear. 'Not fair? Not
what you expected? Or not what you wanted? And it's
Alex, actually. I told you, that's what my friends call
me, and we are friends, I hope?'

His fingers began exploring the ridges of her ribcage
beneath the flimsy material of her bodice, and she heard
herself make an incoherent sort of noise that she hoped
Alexander—Alex—might take as assent to all his questions, for in all honesty she couldn't tell him she didn't
want to feel his arms round her or the warmth of his
mouth as it travelled slowly over her skin.

She swallowed and tried again. 'Not fair,' she wavered.

'Not fair? All's fair at times like these, and if that's
all...'

She heard him chuckle as slowly, inevitably, he turned
her to face him, nodding with satisfaction at the expression in the wide green eyes fixed on his.

'All the same,' he murmured, 'I suppose...' He moved
one hand from its possession of her waist to cup her chin
in gentle fingers. 'As I mentioned before, you haven't
told me anything about yourself, and I wouldn't like to
trespass. Is there someone—someone special, or did you
lose him in Paris? No, don't, Kate. Don't go all prickly,
not now,' he went on softly, sensing her instinctive with-
drawal as her body stiffened in his arms. 'I won't pry,
not if you don't want me to. Just tell me you don't mind
me doing...this...'

He stooped quickly and pressed his mouth to hers in a long, soft kiss, teasing her lips open while the hand that cupped her chin moved slowly to her cheek, then round to the nape of her neck beneath its heavy swing of shining chestnut hair.

'I've been wanting to do this ever since I saw you at Gatwick,' he murmured when at last he lifted his head. 'And don't look so worried.' He bent again to kiss the lines that had appeared between her eyes. 'If you would really rather I didn't kiss you, you only have to tell me. I'm not a complete barbarian, you know, and I am strictly honourable.'

'As befits a knight errant,' Kate said rather shakily.

'Exactly.' Alex kissed her again and although he still held her fast against him she could feel no threat in his embrace. For one wild moment she had wondered just how safe she was here, utterly alone with him and out of reach of any help, but now...one kiss, or two or three, couldn't do any harm, just as long as he didn't expect them to lead anywhere else.

'So—is there a rival for your affections, my lady?' Alex persisted lightly, his eyes searching hers for the answer to his question, and slowly, almost reluctantly, Kate shook her head.

'No, Alex, there isn't anyone, not now.'

To her horror she felt tears well up in her eyes and begin to spill down her cheeks. Hearing herself utter those words out loud made the break-up with Michael seem so much more final. Even to Liz she had only said she had broken off the engagement. To say there was no longer anyone in her life seemed to signal the final disintegration of her long, and, until recently, happy relationship with the man whose wife she had thought she would become.

'I'm sorry, I shouldn't have asked,' Alex said quietly, and his arms relaxed their hold, their strength no longer demanding but comforting as he led her back to the living-room. She dropped into a chair while he fished in his pocket for a spotless white handkerchief which he used to dab very gently at the wetness on her face, then gave to her to hold to her eyes.

'I think it's time I made that coffee,' he said quietly after a moment. 'Unless you'd like me to go?'

'No...no, don't go. Coffee would be lovely—thanks,' Kate told him with a bleak smile as she did her best to pull herself together. She wasn't in the habit of dissolving into tears, especially in front of comparative strangers, and she was cross with herself for her weakness.

'Probably the after-effects of concussion,' Alex told her cheerfully as he left her to go back to the kitchen. 'So what shall it be, Greek or filter?'

'Filter, I think. Perhaps you could show me how to make the other another time?' Kate ventured, wondering whether Alexander would even want to come again after this lamentable show of self-pity, and at the same time realising with a lurch in the pit of her stomach just how much she wanted to see him again.

'Sure,' came the cheerful reply. 'Any time.'

An easy silence, broken only by the sound of Alex's activities in the kitchen, settled between them, and by the time he came back to join her Kate had regained her composure.

Alex made no reference to their previous conversation but smiled across at her as he sat down to wait for the coffee to finish filtering.

'Making coffee is my father's job at home, especially when they want it Greek. It's something my mother's never got the hang of. Probably because she doesn't like it. All those nasty gritty bits,' he added in an exaggerated Scottish accent which made Kate giggle.

'That's better,' Alex approved. 'I like it when you smile. Your dimple shows.'

He got up to come over and kiss the small indentation in her cheek, then vanished back into the kitchen before Kate could protest, emerging moments later with two steaming cups on a tray.

'Is there anything else your mother found hard to adapt to—or your father, for that matter?' Kate enquired as she took a sip of coffee. 'It can't have been easy for either of them to begin with.'

'Do you speak from experience?' Alex enquired with uncustomary irony.

'Observation,' Kate told him. 'The couple who own this house, for example, Penny and Yannis. Actually, it's one of the most successful marriages I know, but there have been times . . .'

Kate put her cup down and leant forward, chuckling reminiscently. 'They had a terrible row once over whether she should go and meet his parents off the train wearing shorts. He wanted her to change into a skirt—it would show more respect, he said.'

'And did she?'

'Did she what?'

'Change into a skirt?'

A new dryness in Alex's voice brought Kate up sharp. He might be half Scots, but the Greek half of him clearly agreed with Yannis.

'Yes, she did,' she admitted. 'But I'm not sure whether . . .' She broke off, biting her lip as she met the mocking glance directed towards her.

'You wouldn't have changed, but then a prickly independent businesswoman with feminist tendencies like yourself is free to please herself.'

A silence, not altogether a comfortable one this time, fell between them, and Kate suddenly remembered the photographs of the mystery girl. Supposing she wasn't Greek, or Scots either . . . Had some fundamental disagreement driven a wedge into her relationship, whatever it was, with Alex? Was that why he had hidden away her likeness at the back of the shelf and, she reflected slowly, felt free to kiss her, Kate, so ardently just now? If only she knew... But instinctively she sensed this was not the occasion to try to find out the answers to these burning questions. She didn't know Alexander well enough, it was as simple as that. His affairs, in whatever sense you cared to use the word, were his alone.

She looked up from a close perusal of her own hands to find Alex's eyes on her, their expression strangely enigmatic.

'As you say, different backgrounds must cause difficulties more conventionally matched couples don't have to contend with, but where there's a will, as my mother would say, and love...'

'And love,' Kate echoed with a sigh Alex was quick to note.

'And talking of parents,' he went on lightly, his face softening, 'what about yours? Do you come from a large family—and are your brothers and sisters as independently minded as you are? If so, your poor mother and father must have had a terrible time trying to keep you all under control.'

'Mine?' Kate's voice was harsh, making Alex's eyebrows rise in surprise. 'My father walked out on my mother and me, and my mother...'

She got up and went over to the window to stare out at the twilit sky. 'You don't know how lucky you are, Alex, to come from a large and happy family.'

All the old longings she'd experienced as a child and back in Alex's living-room swept over her again at the recollection of the picture she'd seen of him surrounded by his parents, brothers and sisters, and she swung round to face him again, a welter of confused and pent-up emotions overwhelming her better judgement.

'Anyway, what's so special about families?' she burst out. 'At least not having one has taught me to be self-sufficient. I'm successful, yes, and independent, and what's so wrong with that? And I've managed it all on my own, with no help from anybody else—certainly not my parents,' she ended with a laugh so bitter that it made Alex wince.

'I'm sorry,' he said quietly. 'If I'd had any idea, of course I'd never have asked.'

He got up from his chair and walked slowly across the room to join her, but made no attempt to touch her as he stood looking down at her, concern on his face mingled with some other emotion she couldn't, and in her present frame of mind didn't want to guess at.

'Maybe one day you'll have——'

Kate flung her head back, her eyes blazing. 'If you're going to say maybe one day I'll have a family of my own, then don't! Children just don't come into my scheme of things, and, anyway, as far as I'm concerned marriage comes before children, and that's something not likely to come my way, not as things stand. And,' she added wildly, 'if you think families are important enough to want to wish one on me, how is it you haven't got one yourself by now?'

There was a sharp intake of breath as though she had inflicted a physical injury on him and she watched the colour ebb from beneath his tan, leaving his complexion strangely grey. He came closer, towering over her, his mouth narrowed into an almost invisible line through which his words were forced out hoarsely.

'I think that is my business, Kate, and nothing to do with anybody else.'

He backed away as though her very proximity were distasteful to him suddenly, reached for the jacket he'd dropped on an upright chair near the door and walked quickly out into the darkness where he turned finally to face her.

'Thank you for going to so much trouble over the meal,' he said quietly. 'The food was delicious.'

Their eyes met as though over an unsurmountable barrier symbolised by the shaft of light from the doorway stabbing down between them and a second later Alex was gone, swallowed up by the shadows beneath the olive trees. She heard his car start up, the gravel scudding up behind the wheels, the fading sound of his engine—then silence . . .

For a long time Kate stood staring out into the night, her thoughts a confused jumble of words and images, until a cool breeze ruffled the thin material of her skirt, making her shiver.

Wrapping her arms tightly round her body, she walked back into the house and pushed the door to with her foot. Then she slumped on the edge of the chair she'd been sitting in and gazed with sightless eyes at the rug on the floor.

In years to come, whenever she saw that particular combination of colours, a rusty brown and dark blue, this moment would come rushing back at her in all its blank misery and anger.

How dared he walk out on her like that? It was all right for him to ask searching questions of her, making assumptions about *her* family, but when the discussion got closer to home he hadn't liked that, had he? Too personal for him, that last remark wrung out of her by her deep-seated resentment and longing.

Her eye fell on his coffee-cup, still half full, and her hand reached out to seize it and dash it to the floor before she remembered just in time that this was someone else's house, and she drew back, trembling with frustrated rage.

Then she leapt to her feet again and began pacing the room as the conversation played itself all over again in her mind like an old-fashioned record stuck in its groove.

She should have seen the direction in which the conversation was heading before it was too late. She hadn't realised she was still so vulnerable on the subject of families. It had been Michael's bombshell which had opened up the old scars she'd thought were healed, and then there had been that photograph...

Kate spent a restless night tossing and turning as each moment of the evening which had begun so enjoyably yet ended in such disaster replayed itself in her mind. Now she would never see Alex again. Not that she wanted to, she told herself fiercely, pummelling her pillow for the umpteenth time. What did she have in common with him?

And yet if they hadn't embarked on that ill-fated discussion, how different things might have turned out then.

With the memory of his gentle kiss on her lips Kate fell into an uneasy sleep only to wake again when it was hardly light, disturbed by the image of Alex's grey, drawn face that had haunted her dreams.

Could she, she wondered bleakly, allowing the first hint of remorse to seep into the edges of her mind, have actually hurt him by that last stinging question? Or had it been his male Greek pride which she had offended?

She knew what store Greek families set by the continuation of the male line and Alex must be thirty at least, maybe thirty-five, and certainly old enough to be married and the father of several children.

Then the penny dropped. Of course—the girl in the photograph! How could she have forgotten her? Alex certainly hadn't, or he wouldn't have stormed out into the night so angrily. But what about those kisses, and his protestations that he was a strictly honourable man? It was hardly honourable to embrace one girl while loving another, as she had more cause than most to know, Kate thought, her mind now in a tumultuous whirl.

Alex's strange behaviour was simply more proof to back up her theory that you couldn't trust any man, no matter how honourable he might seem or claim to be. He was no better—not *much* better, she corrected herself—than Michael.

And to think she'd come here for a rest... Knowing there was no hope now that she'd ever be able to go back to sleep, she got up and went downstairs to make herself another cup of coffee and was brought up sharp by the sight of the filter jug still on the stove and half-full, all the dishes on the table as she had left them the night before.

At least the washing-up would take her mind off Alex, she thought dismally as she ran the water into the bowl. Only it didn't, for every time she picked up a plate or a glass he had used she saw in her mind's eye how he had looked, or smiled, as he had used it, and the cup he had left in the living-room, the one she had wanted to smash to the floor, was halfway to her own lips before she realised what she was doing.

'Stop it!' Kate scolded herself out loud as she plunged the cup into the hot water. 'You're behaving like a moon-struck teenager, and you're an independent, successful career-woman, don't you forget, with a business to run and waiting for you back home.'

She seized a teatowel and began drying the plates with a vigour that threatened to remove the pattern. 'And it's a pity you ever listened to the siren voice of your so-called friend Liz and came here in the first place,' she went on.

But she didn't have to stay here, did she? The place had brought her nothing but ill fortune so far. Money was something she was not short of, so why not move on somewhere else, to a hotel, maybe, where there would be other people to talk to, or at least watch and help her stop her brooding? Company and lots of it was what she needed, not solitude.

Kate felt better now she had come to this decision, and she even began to do some rudimentary packing before getting out the maps to plan her itinerary.

But shouldn't she at least try to put matters straight between herself and Alex before she left? She hated leaving unfinished business of any kind, and in all fairness she couldn't prove any of her suspicions about the girl in the photo. Shouldn't she give him the benefit of all the doubts still simmering in her brain before she bracketed him with Michael?

He had, after all, been very kind to her on more than one occasion, and maybe she did owe him some sort of explanation for her own outburst.

And, as she hadn't a telephone, there was only one thing to do...

On any other day Kate would have enjoyed the drive, with the sparkling blue sea down below her on one side of the road, and on the other the lower slopes of the Taygetus mountains covered at this time of year with green, leafy shrubs and clumps of bright flowers, but she barely noticed any of this as she drove along in increasing trepidation at the prospect of confronting Alexander. Who knew—she certainly didn't—what sort of mood he might be in? He might even refuse to see her...

When she got to his village it was still early, but there was no sign of his car anywhere nor any response from her timid knock at his front door.

She was standing outside, wondering what to do next, when a woman in a nearby house opened a window and smiled at her.

'Kyrios Alexandros?' she queried.

Kate nodded. 'Do you know where he is?'

'Hotel,' the woman told her, gesticulating towards the hill behind them. 'Is at hotel.'

Kate thanked her and with a deep sigh of resignation climbed back into her car. It seemed the Fates had decreed a final meeting between them after all. Well, so be it.

Unless there was another hotel being built on the same headland, this must be the place, she thought minutes later as she rounded a corner and found herself at the end of the road—literally—and on the edge of a large clearing at one end of which was a long, low stone building in the process of construction.

Scattered around was the normal assortment of excavators and lorries and heaps of building materials you would expect to see in such a place, and parked nearby was Alex's car, though there was still no sign of him anywhere.

Feeling painfully conspicuous, Kate sat in her car waiting to see if he would make an appearance, but when after about ten minutes she still hadn't caught so much as a glimpse of him she got out and walked across the site towards the embryonic hotel building perched on the cliff-top.

At least, to judge from the sounds of banging and hammering from inside, she would find somebody there to tell her where he was.

All the activity seemed to be at what she imagined would be the eventual back of the hotel, so she picked her way gingerly round the piles of stone and sacks of cement and then, rounding the corner, she stopped with a gasp of amazement at the spectacular vista spread out in front and below her.

No wonder Alex had chosen this place for his hotel! Forgetting her errand altogether, Kate gazed in delight at the view—the mountains she had been skirting on her way here more visible now, wild and majestic, the domaine of eagles, and towering above the bay below where little fishing boats floated, maybe the boats from which Alex had bought his fish the other day, looking like toys from up here.

Then, stretching out to the horizon, glimmered the sea, a hazy, shifting pattern of blues and greens, scattered here and there with flecks of white as the breeze whipped up the tops of the waves.

CHAPTER FIVE

KATE hadn't gone far before she heard Alex's voice calling abruptly to Kostas, then the sounds of footsteps following behind her—Kostas, presumably, having been given orders to keep an eye on her and make sure she left the site.

Well, she certainly wasn't going to give either man the satisfaction of even a token acknowledgement of her un-wished-for guardian's presence. She straightened her back, and with a defiant toss of her head she marched back to her car, hearing the feet behind her quicken their pace to match hers until she reached the site entrance, when they took a couple of long strides to bring their owner in front of her, blocking her path.

'Alex! I—I thought it was Kostas,' Kate faltered. 'I heard you call out to him——'

'Telling him to mind his own business,' Alex told her urtly. He leant back against Kate's car, arms folded, nd gazed down at her, his expression giving nothing way.

'So why follow me?' Kate demanded hotly, her words unding more peremptory than she might have chosen he tried to counter an unaccountable fluttering in her st. 'You must be very keen to see me leave.'

'ou mentioned leaving, before,' Alex observed imvely. 'Did you mean here——' he gestured towards otel '—or the cottage... or Greece, maybe?'

'e cottage,' Kate told him firmly. 'I think it'
e a change of scene. After all, this is a bi
have the car to explore it in. I may
st of my time here, so—if you'l

Kate stood there, mesmerised, wondering vaguely if you could see the harbour from here, or even Alex's house.

Step by step she wandered towards the edge to get a better view of what lay beneath the overhang, and as she stooped to look at a clump of flowers growing just out of reach, her foot began to slip...

'Oh!'

At the same moment as she felt herself falling, the cry was stifled in her throat and she was dragged back from certain disaster by a strong hand that grabbed her arm with an iron force that almost dislocated her shoulder.

Alex almost flung her away from the treacherously crumbling cliff edge so that she stumbled on to the rough ground, to crouch there, staring up at him and rubbing her bruises.

'You stupid little fool! What do you think you were doing? Trying to kill yourself?'

'Of course not—and did you have to be so rough? You could have broken my arm, pulling at it like that!'

Kate scrambled to her feet and glared at her rescuer, guilt for her carelessness adding fuel to her resentment at his unceremonious handling of her.

'You could have broken a lot more if I hadn't got to you in time,' Alex observed grimly, 'and I've better things to do with my time than watching out for people who've no right to be here in the first place, risking their necks like that. So if you'll excuse me...'

He swung on his heel and began to stride back towards the hotel.

'If it's that dangerous, there should be some warning,' Kate burst out. 'Anybody might be tempted to wander near the edge to look at the view, and there's no barrier.'

'This is private property,' Alex pointed out coldly, 'and all my workmen are fully aware of the dangers on site, but if you had looked a little harder you would have seen that notice.'

He indicated a dusty board stuck into the ground at a crazy angle not many yards away.

Kate gave a snort of derision. 'Not much use, it's all in Greek.'

'This does happen to be Greece,' Alex reminded her in a voice heavy with sarcasm. 'And it's not a tourist area—yet.'

He glared down at Kate who flinched inwardly at the icy gaze directed at her with no hint of the old humour lurking behind the almost colourless eyes.

A construction worker's hard hat covered his thickly curling hair, making him look older and sterner, and his mouth—the mouth that had kissed her so tenderly, Kate remembered with a bitter pang—was tightened into a taut line framed by deeply scored lines that she hadn't noticed before.

'You can be trusted to leave without running into any other trouble, I imagine?' One eyebrow lifted sardonically. 'Or do you need an escort off the site? I'm sure Kostas there would keep an eye on you—you'll forgive me if I don't come myself. I am rather busy at present.'

Kate felt so small as to be practically invisible, especially when she saw that Kostas, a skinny lad taking in every detail of this interesting scene from the hotel doorway, looked as though he ought still to be at school and was barely five feet high into the bargain.

'I can manage perfectly well on my own, thanks,' she retorted, then hesitated. 'There's just one thing——' she began, then stopped with a shake of her head that made her thick, straight hair swing out round her face. 'No, leave it, it's not important. You wouldn't listen, anyway.'

She heard an impatient sigh as she turned to go. 'You may as well tell me now you're here. You must have come all this way for something—or were you just passing? Hardly likely, since the road stops here,' he added ironically before taking a step nearer to loom

almost threateningly over her, dropping his voice so not even the fascinated Kostas could hear him.

'Or had you thought of some other cutting remark you wanted to add to yesterday evening's unwarranted insult?'

Kate could no longer meet the eyes in which undisguised scorn—dislike, even—was so clearly written, and dropped her own gaze to the ground where she scuffed some scattered stones with her toe.

'No,' she said in a low voice, 'I wasn't passing. I came to find you...to say something, before I left.'

'Left?' Alex echoed, and it seemed as though his body tensed at her words, but she dared not raise her eyes.

'I came,' she went on hoarsely, 'to apologise. To te' you I was sorry for what I said last night. It was u' forgivable of me. You got me on the raw, after...w' it doesn't matter now, but that's no excuse for tak' out my feelings on you.'

She ground wretchedly to a halt and took a' breath. 'I'm sorry, Alex,' she said again and sprea' hands helplessly before letting them drop heavily' sides again. 'I won't disturb you any longer. I'' my way.'

Without so much as a glance up at him fo' what she might read on his face, she turned, ' and began walking as steadily as she could ba' her car and new horizons.

She tried to edge past him to open her car door. Alex, however, made no attempt to move, barring her way with his broad frame.

'You've quite made up your mind about that?'

'Quite,' Kate snapped. 'What is there to keep me here? My stay hasn't been what you might call an unqualified success. Even you must agree about that.'

'What happens if you run into more trouble out there in the middle of Greece without anyone to keep an eye on you?' A mocking glint appeared in the grey eyes still fixed unswervingly on Kate's face and she bridled instantly.

'I've spent the whole of my life so far looking after myself quite successfully, thanks, and I'm not intending to alter my lifestyle just on account of one or two mishaps. So, if you'll stand aside, Mr Dimitrakos, I'll be on my way and no further trouble to you.'

'Fine, if that's what you really want.'

Alex unfolded his arms and moved back a couple of paces. 'But there's one thing I want to say before you go—since you took the trouble to come here in the first place.'

Kate paused, her hand on the open door of her car, and looked up curiously at the new, less abrasive, note in his voice.

'Well?'

She saw his mouth curve into a crooked smile. 'It's probably too late to make any difference to your plans, but I thought you ought to know that I do accept the apology you made earlier—on one condition.'

Kate got into the driving seat and then stared up at him coldly. 'There's no need for you to accept it at all,' she said stiffly. 'It was sincerely made, I do assure you, but if there's anything else you feel I ought to have said, or done...grovel, maybe...?'

'No, of course not. You misunderstand me.' Alex turned away, his eyes narrowed against the light as he stared out towards the sea.

'I shouldn't have walked out on you—I'm sorry, Kate. It was just...' He went on standing with his back to her, his shoulders hunched, and Kate knew that something more than offended pride lay both behind his swift disappearance the evening before and his uncharacteristic silence, something she had no means of discovering—yet.

An insane desire swept through her to go over to him and put her arms round him, but she clutched the steering-wheel tightly until he turned and faced her again.

'So can we be friends again?' she asked with a bleak little smile. 'And perhaps it would be best if we forget yesterday evening...?'

'The whole of it, Kate?' Alex came forward to crouch down by the side of the car. 'That seems a pity.'

His voice dropped as his eyes travelled slowly over her face, lingering for a moment on her mouth, and Kate knew by the softening of his expression that he was remembering how she had offered her lips to him, and yielded her body to his embrace. The same memory made her cheeks flush and she averted her eyes quickly away for fear of what he might read in them, but too late, to judge by the twitch at the corners of his mouth.

'Of course we're friends, and I think we should spend the rest of today proving it. It will probably be the last chance, if you're determined to disappear tomorrow. What do you think?'

She should have driven off when she had had the opportunity, a few minutes ago, Kate chided herself, knowing there was no way she could escape now. How could she insist on leaving now? Playing for time, she forced herself to meet the enigmatic grey eyes so close to hers, and gave a reluctant sigh.

'What did you have in mind? Always supposing I'm not in a hurry to be away, of course.'

'Of course,' Alex agreed gravely. 'But you're not, are you? You haven't made any firm plans yet?'

'Not really, no,' Kate confessed, hearing the words of acquiescence forming in her head even before she uttered them. 'No plans.'

'Good.'

Alex rose to his feet in one lithe, easy movement and grinned down at her. 'There's not a lot more I can do here, today, so there's nothing to stop us going off now.'

'Us?' Kate repeated weakly. 'What do you mean, "us"?'

'You and me,' Alex explained patiently. 'I thought I could give you a tour round, taking in Areopolis on the way. I do have some business to do there, and then we could have lunch in a taverna I know. What do you say?'

What could she have said? Kate thought resignedly as she set off for the village to wait for Alex to join her. Without offending him yet again, there was no way she could have refused his offer of a sightseeing trip, and lunch. Did he always manage to get his own way? She ought to be cross that she had allowed herself to be manipulated so easily, but there was something about Alexander Dimitrakos, when he turned the charm on, that made him and his suggestions impossible to resist, and she couldn't deny that her spirits had lifted at the prospect of spending the rest of the day with him—nor that her heart was beating just a little faster.

'Good—you managed the journey without any disaster!'

Kate glared at the cheerful face that appeared in the window of her car as she sat outside his house, but before she could utter the outraged retort forming on her lips Alex was off, striding down the street and calling back at her over his shoulder.

'Stay there a moment. I have to see someone about something.'

Again Kate told herself she ought to resent his constant teasing. It was certainly something she wasn't used to. Michael had never teased her; he was always deadly serious about life, work—everything. Maybe, if he had had more of a sense of humour, if his eyes had danced with that gentle mockery that lit Alex's, even when he had held and kissed her, things might have turned out quite differently.

Kate got out of the car and stood looking out over the sea which lapped gently round the boats moored at the quayside in front of her. How would this day end? she wondered with a lurch in the pit of her stomach. Would Alex want to take her in his arms again, after her outburst yesterday?

Her body shuddered in delicious recollection of being pressed close to his, strong and hard, and she felt her lips soften in anticipation of his kisses. Supposing... supposing he did want to resume that embrace where they had left off? Where would that lead? And if he wanted to make love to her, what would—should—her response be?

And if... and if...? But what was the use of speculating? Kate shook her head in confusion and wrapped her arms round her slim frame as though to protect it from sensations she had vowed she would never seek to experience again.

'You can't be feeling cold—unless you're ill again?'

Kate swung round at the sound of Alex's voice just behind her and dropped her arms to her sides, smiling sheepishly.

'No, I'm not cold,' she assured him. 'Just—what do they say?—someone walking over my grave.'

She saw the familiar teasing glint fade from Alex's eyes as he came up to stand beside her, quite close, but making no attempt to touch her.

'Forget that someone, just for today,' he said quietly. 'Simply relax and try to enjoy yourself. That's why you're here, isn't it?'

Kate nodded slowly.

'Right, come on, then, or we won't have time to see anything.'

He took her by the hand and led her to his own car. 'So, a guided tour and some lunch, and then—well, we'll see where our fancy takes us, shall we?'

There was no hint of a hidden meaning either in his tone or on his face and Kate settled back in her seat with a little sigh of contentment to enjoy the ride.

Alex dropped her near the centre of Areopolis, pointing out the taverna where they would be lunching and saying he would meet her there in about an hour.

'You'll be all right till then? No, don't prickle,' he grinned, 'it was only a polite question, not an aspersion on your ability to look after yourself. Look—there's an interesting little church over there. It's got some amazing frescoes—oh, and if you trip over a load of shopping piled up outside, don't worry that it's been forgotten. People leave it there to be cared for by the local saint while they go off and do other things.'

He turned the car and disappeared down one of the little alleys leading off what was presumably the main shopping street, the usual jumble of houses and shops with, at one end, the church to which he had referred. Sure enough, outside it was indeed an assortment of plastic bags and baskets left by the trusting shoppers.

This endearing sight, combined with the peaceful atmosphere inside the dark little building, raised Kate's spirits, and she emerged into the daylight feeling the tensions that had been haunting her ever since her breakup with Michael ease gradually from her mind, almost as though, she thought fancifully, she had left her own burden in the saint's care along with the bags of vegetables.

She sauntered off, not knowing where she was going, happy just to drift along enjoying the sights and sounds of this unremarkable yet attractive little town. She wandered along narrow alleys whose high walls later in the year would be bright with climbing plants, lost in a heedless reverie until the delicious smell of freshly baked bread from a bakery nearby reminded her first that she was hungry, then about her lunch-date with Alex.

She quickened her pace, fearing she would be late, until she brought herself up sharply with a grin. This was Greece, wasn't it, where every waiter's cheerful 'coming right away' meant in fifteen or twenty minutes at least. So, why hurry? Time was not important here, and today it was something she and Alex had plenty of.

'I hope you haven't been waiting long,' she told him when she got back to the taverna to find him already there, leaning against the wall and idly watching the world go by. 'I'm sorry, but I wandered off and forgot the time,' she added not very apologetically.

Alex straightened up and smiled. 'Not long. So, tell me where you've been.'

He led the way through the taverna to a little open-air terrace at the back, with Kate chatting happily about what she'd seen on her brief tour round the town, but after they'd sat down and were waiting for their first course to arrive she found it increasingly difficult to continue this carefree and casual conversation as though nothing had happened.

She reached for some bread and began breaking off little pieces, arranging them round the edge of her plate with fierce concentration.

'About last night,' she began awkwardly, her face averted, 'I ought——'

'I thought we'd agreed to forget all that,' Alex interrupted her gently. 'We've both admitted we said things that maybe would have been best left unsaid. Wouldn't it be as well to leave it at that?'

Kate raised troubled eyes to his. 'I expect so, but I just wanted to explain... It all happened a long time ago, what I told you, and I thought it didn't matter any more, that I'd put it all behind me. Evidently I was wrong, though, and you got the full force of feelings I'd been bottling up for ages.'

She gave him a wan smile. 'It's no excuse, I know that, but various things have happened recently to upset the emotional applecart, and then when you suggested I might want a family of my own, to compensate...'

Her voice trailed away as Alex reached across the table and covered her hand with his. 'I told you, we'll forget it,' he said quietly. 'I expect there are potential volcanos in most people's lives waiting to erupt, given the right trigger.'

Kate saw him frown and the lines framing his mouth deepen as they had done during their altercation earlier that morning, but she had no opportunity to try even to discover the reason, as the waiter arrived just then with their first course and the momentary bleakness passed as swiftly as it had appeared.

'So let me tell you about my hotel,' Alex offered, passing her the salad. 'You were suitably impressed with the view, I take it? Almost carried away, in fact.'

His eyes glinted wickedly and Kate found herself disarmed all over again by his good-humoured banter which made her forget, for the time being at least, the doubts and uncertainties that had kept her awake half the night and sent her in search of Alex early that morning.

'I'll have to reserve judgement on the building itself until it's completed,' she told him, 'but if it's anything like the Alexandros...'

'Good heavens, Kate!' Alex ejaculated scornfully. 'It's not going to be anything like the Alexandros. Not in the same class at all.' He stabbed ferociously at a piece of tomato as he glared at her.

'I'm sorry,' Kate said meekly. 'No offence meant, but the Alexandros was actually very comfortable, even if the views from it weren't quite so spectacular.'

'So I should hope—I hope all my hotels are comfortable, but this one is going to be in a class of its own—the very top, and I mean *top*,' he said emphatically. 'I'm aiming for it to be the most luxurious hotel in the whole of Greece.'

'I see.' Kate was impressed. 'You said "all my hotels" just now,' she went on curiously. 'How many hotels do you own, then?'

'Oh, let's see.' Alex leant back in his chair and counted slowly on his fingers. 'There's this one—and I haven't thought of a name yet, if you've any bright ideas—and the Alexandros, of course, the Apollo at Delphi, the Zeus, another Alexandros near Thessaloniki...I think that's the lot. Then of course I have two or three apartment blocks, one in Athens, one in Corinth——'

'Stop, stop!' Kate cried in mock alarm. 'I can't take any more in. And to think how pleased I've been with myself for having two boutiques...' She shook her head ruefully. 'How pathetic you must have thought my meagre achievement.'

'Not at all,' Alex declared. 'I don't know how old you are, and I wouldn't presume to ask, but think how many more shops you'll have by the time you're my age—a whole chain of them, I shouldn't wonder. Unless, of course,' he added almost as an afterthought, 'something happens to change the direction of your life altogether. You never know...'

Kate flashed him a warning glance, knowing full well what he was referring to. 'Very unlikely. I've had my fingers burnt once, and that's enough for me.'

She turned her attention ostentatiously to her meal, finishing the *souvlaki* with relish, then leaning back in her chair with a contented sigh.

'That was excellent,' she told Alex. 'I don't think I could eat anything more for at least a week.'

Alex pulled a wry face. 'That's a pity. I had thought...no, never mind. It'll keep, for now. Maybe exercise is what you need, in that case,' he went on, getting to his feet and holding out his hand to Kate to pull her out of her chair. 'There's something you must see before we leave here—the statue of our great hero. Unless you've seen him already? If you had, though, I'm sure you'd have mentioned him. He's pretty impressive.'

'Here?' Kate queried.

'The great Mavromichalis. A resistance leader, I suppose you'd call him nowadays. The man who started the revolt against the occupying Turks. You couldn't miss him if you've been in the square.'

Kate wrinkled her brow. 'No, I went off down the main street to those little alleyways at the bottom. I'm sure I never saw a statue, only churches.'

'Right, come on, then.'

Alex settled the bill and led Kate out into the street again; then, rounding the corner, he said proudly, 'There he is. What d'you think?'

'My goodness!' Kate exclaimed in awe as she gazed up at the huge figure on his plinth, booted and mustachioed, and with one hand resting on a great, curved sword. 'Pretty impressive, just as you said.'

'And not much like your Michael, I guess,' Alex murmured quietly behind her.

Kate swung round, caught completely off guard. '*My* Michael? But I've never...how did you know?'

'I didn't, it was a guess. When I mentioned Black Michael yesterday you reacted, probably quite unconsciously, but I knew the name must mean something to you. Then there were those tears when I blundered in with my question about whether there was anyone special in your life...I just put two and two together, that's all. I'm sorry, maybe I shouldn't have said anything.'

Kate went on staring at the fierce, implacable face of the freedom fighter gazing out over her head and gave a faint smile.

'No, he doesn't look in the least like my Michael, as you call him. Only he isn't mine, not any more. That's why...'

Her voice faltered a little and she felt Alex's arm go round her shoulders.

'That's why I came away, to try and forget him—the whole thing.'

Alex turned her gently to face him. 'Do you want to talk about it? It can help sometimes.'

For a second Kate was tempted to tell him everything, even about Carol and the baby.

'I...' she began, then she shook her head. 'No, I don't think so. I don't want to be reminded of him, or of what he did, especially not just now. Anyway,' she went on brightly, 'isn't it time you told me something about yourself—more than just how many hotels you own? What about your girlfriends? Is there anyone special— the girl in the photograph, for instance? Who is she? Wouldn't she mind you taking me out to lunch—and everything?'

The question was out before she could prevent it and immediately she wished she had left it unasked. Alex had been holding her arm but now he dropped it to stare with narrowed eyes across the busy square, plunging his hands deep into his pockets, and when he turned back to her the contours of his face had become suddenly angular, as though carved from unyielding stone.

'That girl,' he said slowly, his voice so harsh it made Kate wince, 'needn't matter to you. I can assure you of that, and I'm sorry you think I'm the sort of man who would kiss a girl as I kissed you if I already...'

He broke off and Kate's cheeks warmed under the sudden intensity of his gaze. 'If you don't mind, I'd rather not speak about her again. What's past is past.'

Without another word he led the way back to the car with Kate following behind him not knowing what to make of Alex's curt dismissal of her innocent enquiry. If the girl didn't matter, why keep her picture in his wallet? He'd given her no clue, and she certainly couldn't ask him again. There was only one shred of comfort—Alex was unattached.

For a while Alex was so uncharacteristically quiet that Kate assumed that everything was now irrevocably over between them and that he would be driving her straight back to the village to collect her car, but to her surprise he began by setting off in the opposite direction, heading south instead of north.

'So where are we going now?' she asked eventually, breaking the uneasy silence that enveloped them.

'Just round and about, I thought.' Alex changed gear to negotiate a steep bend. 'I thought I'd show you a few of my favourite villages before we go back, but I don't want to be too late getting home, if you don't mind.'

'No, of course not,' Kate agreed, trying not to show the disappointment she felt in her voice. Somehow she'd anticipated spending the whole day and evening too with Alex, though of course now that was out of the question. There was no reason why he would feel the same about her as he had before she'd begun to pry into his private life.

To compensate for what she now felt sure Alex must see as an unwarrantable intrusion on her part, Kate forced herself to make bright and interested comments on the places he was showing her, asking what she hoped were intelligent questions to keep him talking and make him think she was really appreciative of his efforts on her behalf.

'Today has been nice,' she told him enthusiastically when he finally headed home and turned off on to the by now familiar corkscrewing road down to his village. A surreptitious glance at her watch told her it was only five o'clock, but clearly Alex had decided enough was enough. He had not even suggested that they might spend the evening together, she thought miserably.

'It was very good of you to give up so much time to showing me around,' she persevered gamely. 'I did appreciate it, truly.'

Alex frowned as he manoeuvred the car round a particularly sharp bend, then shot her a suspicious look.

'That sounds very stiff and formal,' he commented with an ironic lift of his eyebrows. 'I had hoped you might have actually enjoyed the day, rather than merely appreciating it.'

'Of course I did,' Kate protested. 'It's just—oh, I don't know...' She hesitated, then ploughed on doggedly, 'You seemed so anxious to get back, I thought you were still cross with me for asking...you know,' she ground to a halt, spreading her hands helplessly. 'And you might have been regretting spending so much time showing me round. After all, you only invited me out on an impulse, didn't you?'

'Maybe,' Alex admitted, 'but some impulses can be worth acting on. You just have to take the risk.'

The corners of his mouth moved, but he didn't expand on the point. 'As it happens, I did have to get back for a particular reason, but it has nothing to do with any regrets at how I—we—have spent the day, I promise you. Or not directly,' he mysteriously added with a half-smile more to himself than to Kate which left her feeling unsettled and still with that sense of disappointment nagging at her. To have to return to her empty cottage now would be such an anticlimax. She should have stuck to her guns earlier in the day and left as she had planned to do.

Alex brought the car to a halt just behind hers and got quickly out to open the passenger door for her.

This was it, then. The end of a beautiful friendship, let alone anything else—not that she wanted anything else, Kate reminded herself severely as she, too, climbed out to stand looking up at him. There were clearly too many complications in both their lives.

'Thanks again for the tour,' she said with forced lightness, 'and for the lunch, too. And let me know when the hotel's finished, won't you? I'll tell all my friends to come and stay, and admire Black Michael, too.'

She gave a brittle little laugh and held out her hand.

'You're going, then?' Alex enquired, staring at her hand but making no attempt to take it in his. Instead, he walked round to the boot which he opened, then took out a couple of well-filled plastic carrier bags containing food, so far as Kate could see.

'Now that's a pity,' he continued, eyeing her speculatively, 'because I had other plans for the rest of the day. Still, if you're in a hurry to go...'

He shut the car and turned as though to leave her, carrying his purchases towards his house.

'Other plans...' Kate echoed, her voice not quite as steady as she might have wished. 'But I thought you had something already arranged—something you had to get back here for.'

'So I do, but you never asked what that arrangement was,' Alex observed as he disappeared through his front door.

'Your arrangements aren't any of my business,' Kate protested, following him. 'I wouldn't presume to ask.'

'Ah, but that's where you're wrong, this time,' Alex grinned. 'They're very much your business, as it happens—or at least that was what I had hoped.'

He crossed the road and put his fingers to his mouth, producing a strident whistle which was answered by a shout from a man standing a hundred yards or so away along the quayside. Alex called out something, and the man nodded vigorously, pointing to a neat, white-painted boat moored nearby. Alex nodded in acknowledgement and turned to Kate, who was watching this exchange with a certain amount of mystification.

'Right, that's all settled,' Alex said with satisfaction. 'Everything's ready and now it all depends...' He paused to study Kate's appearance with a slight frown. 'Let's see—jeans, trainers, shirt, that's OK, but you might need something warmer later on. Have you got a sweater with you?'

'I've got a sweatshirt in the car,' Kate told him, 'but why...?' She stared at him, perplexed, then the penny dropped. 'That boat—are you—are we...?'

Alex nodded. 'I did promise to take you out in a boat before you left, if you remember, and this seems to be the last chance I'll get, if you're set on leaving to-morrow. So, will you come? Or do you want to go home now? It's up to you.'

'I really ought to go back and finish my packing,' Kate began not very convincingly, yet feeling instinctively she should at least put up a show of independence until she met the mocking glint on Alex's face.

'I can't think of anything nicer,' she heard herself saying with a lamentable show of eagerness, and now here she was, only minutes later, chugging quietly across the bay, having let herself be hijacked yet again, and willingly, by the man sitting smiling at her from the stern of the little fishing boat.

As their eyes met and held in a companionable silence another remark came back to Kate, one Alex had made at the same time as his promise to take her on a boat trip and one she would rather not have remembered just at this precise moment. She only hoped Alex had forgotten it along with the blush his words had painted on her cheeks.

'There's only one way,' he had said, 'to appreciate these fish properly, and that's cooked on an open fire on a beach miles from anywhere—preferably with a beautiful girl as the sun is going down over the sea.' And he had added, 'It will be an experience you'll never forget.'

A tremor ran through Kate's body. She must have been crazy to agree to come with Alex—not that she couldn't trust him. But could she trust herself?

CHAPTER SIX

ALMOST imperceptibly the day slipped into evening as their boat moved quietly across the bay whose waters even at this time of year were so translucently blue that Kate felt sure she'd be able to see the bottom if she peered closely enough.

'Hey, keep still,' Alex warned her as she leant perilously over the side of the boat. 'I don't want to have to add life-saving to my list of good deeds on your behalf. Not in these waters, anyway. They're pretty cold, I warn you.'

'Too cold for a swim?'

'Definitely,' came the firm reply. 'And I'm not being over-protective, either. I wouldn't swim here myself, though there is a little bay I know where you can bathe almost all the year round. Not that I'll have the opportunity to show you now, will I? Not if you're leaving us tomorrow.'

'No,' Kate agreed brightly, desperately trying to suppress the image that surfaced in her mind of Alex's strong, muscular frame clad only in bathing shorts—poised to dive, or stretched out on a sunny beach, and herself lying by his side...

She dropped her gaze quickly to study the plastic carriers Alex had brought from Areopolis, now stowed away at her feet together with a rug, and a motley collection of other containers.

'What's in all those bags?' she enquired with studied casualness. 'There seems an awful lot just for two—oh, where are we going now?'

Alex didn't answer for a moment as he altered course to steer round an outcrop of rock before heading out into the open sea beyond the bay. His face creased into a smile as he observed the anxious expression on Kate's face.

'Don't worry, I'm not kidnapping you. I'm no white slaver—too much trouble, for one thing. Imagine keeping all those nubile girls in order...not to mention the temptations on hand.'

His grin widened at the outraged glare Kate directed at him, then he slowed the engine and pointed back the way they had come.

'Look—there's my hotel,' he told her proudly. 'Over on the headland, where I rescued you from a premature end this morning.'

Kate ignored this remark and concentrated instead on the view of the half-finished building on the cliff-top behind them. It was going to be extremely attractive, she could see that even at this stage, but when she gazed at the wild and desolate hills with the distant village hugging the shoreline, she couldn't help feeling a pang of regret that its rugged peace was about to be irrevocably disturbed for ever.

'It really is a spectacular site you've chosen,' she admitted, 'although——'

'Although what?' Alex demanded, quick to seize on any hint of criticism. 'What's wrong with it? You don't mean to tell me you think it's—what did Prince Charles call that place that aroused his royal displeasure? A carbuncle?'

Kate laughed. 'No, it's not that—not even a pimple! I'm sure as a building it's going to be quite beautiful, only I think I might prefer that mountain bare as it is with just the village at its foot. It's so romantic in its own way.'

'That village, romantic or not, would be almost deserted by now,' Alex pointed out drily, 'if it weren't for ventures like mine. Why else do you think my father had to emigrate to find work? Things haven't changed. There just isn't enough to support the people round here, you only have to look around.'

There was no opportunity to pursue this discussion just at this moment as Alex rounded the headland and the boat began to roll in the stronger waves of the open sea which slapped at the wooden sides and sprayed up into Kate's face until he turned in again towards the coast and headed for a small sandy cove sheltered by the rocks.

Alex cut the engine so that they drifted in for the last few metres while he took his shoes off and rolled up the legs of his jeans.

'You stay where you are while I pull us in,' he ordered Kate, jumping over the side into the knee-deep water to adjust the outboard motor before dragging the boat up the beach as far as he could. Then, just as Kate was about to climb out, and giving her no time to protest, he strode round and grasped her round the middle, lifting her over the side to deposit her gently on the sand.

Was it her imagination, or did he go on holding her just a moment or two longer than he needed to? There was certainly no imagining the teasing light in his eyes as he smiled down at her, anticipating her response to his gallantry.

'I know, you're going to tell me you could have got out quite safely on your own,' he said airily.

'And so I could,' she retorted. 'I'm not completely helpless, you know.'

'Oh, I do know.' She felt Alex's strong fingers tighten on her waist. 'But I wouldn't have enjoyed that half as much.'

He released her reluctantly, his smile broadening at her half-feigned expression of outrage before he turned back to the boat to start unloading it. He handed Kate the rug.

'Put this on the ground over there,' he told her, pointing up the beach.

'Aye, aye, Captain,' Kate replied with a meekness that surprised herself then, wondering vaguely how it was she always seemed to accept his orders without so much as a demur, she walked up the sand to place the rug where he had indicated. She squatted down beside a ring of blackened stones and stared curiously at the heap of old ash which she prodded with a charred stick lying nearby.

'Soon get that going,' Alex remarked, rummaging in one of the bags he'd just deposited on the ground beside her. After setting light to some bundles of dried twigs he began arranging charcoal on the top with a deftness born of long practice, and in what seemed no time at all he had a hot fire glowing in his fireplace.

He placed a metal grille over this and then from a coolbox brought out two silvery fish, already cleaned and gutted, which he laid on top and brushed lightly with some olive oil.

'There you are,' he said smugly. 'How's that for an al fresco meal? Simple, I grant you, but quite perfect, I reckon.'

Kate sat up and hugged her knees, fixing him with wide, serious eyes. 'I'm a bit disappointed, actually.'

'Oh? How so?' Alex seemed quite taken aback. 'What more could you need? You must admit the setting's original, and as romantic as you could wish.'

'The setting's fine,' Kate agreed, 'but I did imagine you'd actually be catching the fish yourself. These—' she nodded towards the home-made barbecue '—I guess you bought in Areopolis, or got from your friend back in the village. I'm sure they'll be delicious,' she went on hastily, not wanting to offend him, 'but not the same as if they'd come straight out of the sea.'

Alex stretched out a long arm for yet another bag from which emerged a bottle of wine and two glasses.

'I did think of that,' he admitted, 'but I decided to make sure of our supper rather than risk us going hungry. This time, anyway, as I didn't have long to prepare. If you were staying on, of course, it would be different. We could spend the whole day fishing, swimming...drinking wine...making l——'

'Is that for me?' Kate almost snatched one of the glasses from Alex's hand, spilling a drop of the golden coloured liquid on the rug in her anxiety to prevent him saying the words she didn't want to hear, not even half-seriously.

Alex's mouth twitched and his eyes danced but all he said was, 'You do like retsina, I hope?'

Kate sniffed the wine doubtfully. 'Well, actually, I don't, not very much.'

'Too bad,' her host countered unsympathetically. 'Wait till you've tasted this—and it's the only thing to drink in the circumstances, I promise you. Here, have some bread. Dimitri's wife made it specially.'

'Dimitri?' Kate enquired.

'The chap who looks after my boat for me when I'm away. His wife, another Maria, is the best bread maker for miles around.'

Kate bit into the chunk he handed her then sipped gingerly at the retsina, and her face lit up.

'This is delicious!' she exclaimed in surprise. 'Quite unlike what I've had before, and with the bread...'

She lay back on the rug, propped up by her elbows, and only when she saw Alex's eyes slide over her body, lingering on the upthrust curves of her breasts beneath the thin material of her shirt, was she assailed by sudden doubts about his true motives in bringing her to this deserted spot. Colouring faintly, she quickly sat up again and pulled as unobtrusively as she could at the rather too skimpy garment in an effort to hide the shape of the body beneath, but not unobtrusively enough to hide the gesture from Alex's ever watchful, amused gaze.

He reached out and touched her gently on the arm, the warmth of his fingers enough to send a tremor of something she didn't want to acknowledge go rushing along her nerve ends.

'You can't stop me looking at you, Kate,' he said softly. 'You are a very beautiful girl, but looking is as far as it will go...well, maybe not quite as far,' he added airily, 'but I didn't bring you here for any nefarious purpose. Just an evening to remember. Now, are those fish ready yet?'

In a rather confused state Kate watched Alex slide the fish on to two plates, one of which he placed on the ground before her with a flourish, together with a dish of Greek salad which materialised from yet another container, and she smiled rather unsteadily at him.

'Do you come here often, Mr Dimitrakos?' she asked lightly in a determined attempt to steer the conversation away from the rather too dangerous waters into which they had been venturing.

'As often as I can, Miss Penwarden. It's my favourite eating place, secluded and highly exclusive, as you may have observed. And the food is of a standard unlikely to be equalled anywhere in the area.'

'Even at that superior hotel you showed me earlier?' Kate enquired, laughter in her voice.

'Even there,' Alex informed her gravely. 'And what's more, I shall make sure none of the guests at that particular establishment ever gets to hear of it. This place is strictly private, and I am very particular who I invite here. Tell me, what do you think of the cuisine?'

Kate ate another forkful of grilled fish and savoured its delicate flavour as she tried to banish from her mind the image of all the other girls—including the one in the photograph—whom Alex had brought here to share a meal cooked over this fire.

'First class, I'd say, both the ingredients and the cooking. In fact,' she went on after a moment, 'I can't remember a meal I've ever enjoyed more.'

'So you're glad you didn't obey your first instincts and take off into the blue this morning—or go back and do your packing?'

Kate sighed as she made her reluctant confession. 'Yes, I'm glad, although...' she added, her suspicions aroused by the quizzical lift of Alex's eyebrow.

'Although?' he prompted her.

'Although if you think you're going to dissuade me again from leaving, you're going to be disappointed. I really shall be going tomorrow.'

'Of course,' Alex murmured, eyeing her over the rim of his glass. 'I never imagined you'd change your mind again. You're a very determined girl, I've learnt that much about you at least.'

He drained his glass and twirled it thoughtfully between his fingers. 'But in spite of all you've already told me I feel somehow there's still a lot to discover about you, Miss Penwarden—the real Kate Penwarden, I mean, not the independent, rather prickly career woman you like everyone to think you are.'

Kate opened her mouth to remonstrate, but some softening of Alex's ruggedly handsome face made her keep back the sharp retort hovering on her lips.

Instead, she got up and walked slowly to the water's edge, feeling his eyes on her, but knowing instinctively that he wouldn't follow her unless she wanted him to. He seemed to have an innate understanding of her that she'd never experienced before, not even with Michael, and it was both disturbing and at the same time oddly comforting. But even now there was something deep within her that held her back from wanting to tell him the whole truth about her relationship with Michael.

She stared out to the horizon where the sun was setting, a deep red globe poised on the sea's rim making streaks of crimson ripple across the water. It was so quiet, the only sound she could hear was the lapping of the tiny waves at her feet.

'So who is this Michael who has the power still to make you so unhappy?'

Alex's deep voice broke the silence and for a moment Kate stayed where she was, reluctant to let loose all the memories still banked down below the surface of her mind, but she turned at last, and, as though impelled by some irresistible force, walked back to join him.

She sat on the farthest edge of the rug, knees hunched beneath her chin, and began to speak in a dull monotone.

'Michael was my fiancé, but we—I—broke it off about a month ago. After three years,' she added gratingly.

'Three years,' Alex murmured pensively. 'That's a long time to wait. I know I couldn't wait that long for a girl I really loved.'

Kate made no comment, but her fingers dug into the sand and began making a miniature castle, and Alex watched, fascinated, as she demolished it with one vicious swipe and swung round to face him.

'He wanted—expected—certain things I couldn't commit myself to, so in the end he found someone else who could,' she said bluntly, staring intently at the ruins of her castle. 'You see, I've always felt that everything should happen in the right order—you fall in love, get engaged, then marry. Only then do you give yourselves to one another, and afterwards, those who want a family...'

She coloured slightly as her voice faded away. 'I expect you think I'm as old-fashioned as Michael did,' she went on bleakly after a while. 'He wasn't prepared to wait, you see, or that was his excuse, and when he and Carol—his secretary—were together in Paris...'

'Ah—Paris. Now I see,' Alex murmured almost to himself. He longed to reach out and take Kate in his arms to comfort her but knew if he did, or even said any more, this moment of painful truth would vanish for ever, so he waited patiently for her to continue, but she shook her head as though sensing his thoughts. Never would she be able to speak to anyone, not even Alex, about the child Michael and Carol had conceived, the ultimate betrayal, nor about those terrible final words Michael had flung at her, so doubly cruel in the circumstances.

'So now you know.' She hugged her knees and bent her head to rest her forehead on them so that a shining chestnut curtain fell across her cheeks, hiding her face from the man sitting so still as he listened and watched.

A shadow clouded his own eyes, then very gently he touched her on the shoulder.

'I'm so sorry,' he said in a low voice. 'Maybe I shouldn't have asked, but I'm glad I did. I needed to know.'

His hand moved from her shoulder to push back her hair and to her horror Kate felt tears well up in her eyes and begin to trickle down her cheeks, just as they had the evening before. She tried to hide them, turning her head away, but unchecked they began dropping on to her bare arm.

Without another word he drew her towards him, tilting her head back with gentle fingers which moved to touch her cheek. Then with a little smile he put them to his lips.

'Salt,' he said softly. 'Salt as the sea, but there's no need to cry, sweetheart. I won't ask any more questions, I promise, not if you don't want to talk about it.'

Kate shook her head helplessly, feeling the tears threaten again at his unexpected endearment.

'It's not that,' she quavered. 'I couldn't believe he could do that to me, not after all we'd meant, or all I'd thought we'd meant to one another. We had been happy, I did think we really loved one another. But after all those years, the sudden realisation that he could have an affair with another woman, and that I didn't know him at all—I still can't take it in,' she ended, not quite steadily.

She buried her face against Alex's broad chest as his arms went tightly round her to hold her close until she felt her tension begin to ease.

'Better to discover the truth about him before it was too late,' he commented gently. 'And the pain will fade in time, I promise you.'

A new note in his voice made Kate look round at him, but his expression was giving nothing away and she felt too drained to try to discover what precise meaning lay behind his words. 'I didn't tell you all this to make you feel sorry for me,' she said dully. 'As you say, it will all pass in time. Everything does.'

'Not everything.'

Kate felt his fingers tighten convulsively round her own and she looked up, startled, into his face, recognising with a shiver of anticipation the unmistakable gleam of hunger in the grey eyes searching her own.

'And I didn't bring you here this evening out of pity. Michael mustn't be allowed to spoil what I promised you would be an unforgettable evening, must he? He belongs to the past, but the present...here—now...is ours.'

Still holding tightly on to her hand, he got to his feet and drew her after him. Then he pulled her tightly against him and she felt his hands slide slowly up her back to curve round the slender stem of her neck.

'And the here and now is what I have to settle for, isn't it? So I must use what time I have...'

She just had time to catch the glint in his eyes as his head bent over hers, and the lips that brushed across her mouth were as warm and sensuous as they had been on that other occasion—could it have been only yesterday? she wondered, in a kind of daze.

Hardly aware of what she was doing, she found herself leaning against him, feeling her body melt with sudden and dizzying ecstasy as he took full possession of her mouth while his hands began their own slow voyage of discovery.

Gentle fingertips caressed the little hollow beneath her ear, travelled down her neck to her shoulder, stroking the softness of her upper arms before sliding beneath them to rest against the swell of her breasts.

Kate's knees turned to jelly as he swiftly stooped to kiss her throat, bent lower to find the tautened curves cupped in his hands, making her back arch in an instinctive response that made her stomach contract in a spasm of desire.

Her hands reached out to touch the black, springing hair, cradling his head against her...

'No!' she cried suddenly, struggling free to stand back from him as the full realisation of what was happening struck her. 'No, Alex, you promised. You said you—we—hadn't come here for...'

Her words trailed away as she dropped her gaze, fearful of uttering the actual words.

'For lovemaking, you were going to say.' Alex's voice was low. 'No, you're right, and I'm sorry. I forgot myself, and your principles.'

Kate's head whipped back, but there was no hint of mockery on his expression as he turned to face the sea, the set of his shoulders giving Kate no clue as to his innermost feelings.

'You...I didn't mean...' she began, but he moved his hand dismissively.

'It's your fault if I overstepped the mark,' he said lightly. 'A man would have to be made of iron not to be led astray here, in this place, alone with a girl as beautiful as you are.'

He gave a heavy sigh and thrust his hands deep into his pockets and, although Kate had no idea whether he was making fun of her or not, again, as she had done on the cliff-top that morning, she had to suppress an almost overpowering urge to put her arms round him. The other, deeper urge that yearned for his arms to embrace her, and his lips to crush hers, she dared not even contemplate.

An affair, however short and casual, did not figure in her plans, not with the memory of one unhappy relationship still so fresh in her memory.

She walked slowly back to the crumpled rug and the remains of their meal, which she began packing away, trying her best to ignore the acceleration of her pulses as she heard Alex's approaching footsteps. Maybe, she thought with a flicker of hope that refused to be quenched, he had decided to take no notice of her protests.

She kept her head studiously averted as he crouched down beside her and her heart leapt as he reached out to push aside the heavy locks of hair falling across her cheek.

'It wasn't quite one-sided, was it?' he murmured with the old laughter in his voice. 'When I held you in my arms, just for a moment, you felt something, didn't you?'

He leant forward and kissed her gently. 'Don't deny yourself every possibility for happiness, Kate. Don't imprison the warm, responsive girl you really are for ever just because of what happened between you and Michael. I know the pain's still there, but there are more ways of easing it than denying life to all other feelings. Even a little light dalliance can be a tonic, you know, in certain circumstances.'

In certain circumstances and with certain men, maybe, Kate thought several hours later as she sat up in bed, propped up by pillows and pretending to read, but the print slipped, unread, down the page, as she went over yet again all the events of what had turned out to be a very strange and disturbing day.

The return journey from Alex's secluded cove had been uneventful, and if either of them had any regrets at how the evening had ended they remained unspoken. Alex had left Kate at her front door with no more than the most casual of kisses, hardly more than a peck on the cheek.

'Mind how you go,' he'd said lightly as he turned to go, dismissing her words of thanks with a shrug. 'Look after yourself while there isn't anyone else to do it. I hope things sort themselves out for you.'

And that was that. No more teasing remarks to persuade her to stay on, not even a last embrace. Just a brief smile and a wave and he was gone out of her life forever.

He might have tried a bit harder, a perverse feminine streak deep within her whispered in her ear. He didn't have to leave quite so readily, though of course she wouldn't have given in to any further persuasion on his part to postpone her departure. She really was going to leave tomorrow, but it would have been nice to have felt he wanted her to stay.

Maybe he didn't, though. The thought stabbed through her cold as steel.

Those moments when he had held and caressed her had probably been nothing but mere 'dalliance'—his word—as far as he was concerned, but Kate knew only too well that, had she not escaped from his arms, that dalliance might so easily have become something more.

Her hand stole to her lips which Alex had pressed so ardently with his out there beneath the twilit sky, and her breasts ached for the touch of his warm, strong hands that had rested against them. With a futile gesture, as though to push aside even the memory of the sensation they had aroused in her body, she leapt out of bed to go and stand by the open window.

'For goodness' sake!' she cried out loud in self-disgust. 'Stop behaving like a lovesick teenager. You don't mean anything to him—not anything!'

Or else why, she asked herself again, had he left so abruptly without so much as a suggestion that he might come into the house with her, even for an innocent coffee?

Had all his protestations about wanting to find out more about the real her been nothing but an excuse to get out in his boat for a spot of 'dalliance' on that deserted beach which had no doubt been the setting for countless other such assignations?

Kate leant her elbows on the windowsill and rested her chin on her cupped hands as she gazed out at the night sky now studded with stars, the same stars that would be shining down on Alex, who was no doubt asleep with no thought of her to trouble his dreams.

The image of his dark, handsome face rose up in her mind and she saw as clearly as though he were actually present those humorous grey eyes studying her with— what? Go on, she told herself ruthlessly, be honest.

It wasn't only casual appraisal of her attractions that she read on his features, either now, in her imagination, or in reality; nor the pity he had disclaimed; but true concern for her, Kate Penwarden, as she really was, prickles and all.

Those accusations she had been mentally heaping on him had been unfair, she confessed wretchedly to herself, and, if he had felt rejected, who could blame him?

She remembered now those rare moments when she had seen that strangely bleak expression shadow his eyes, the quickly disguised remark hinting at some past unhappiness. That girl in the photographs was the cause, she was sure, but after that fierce warning not to mention her again she'd taken Alex at his word. Perhaps she should have tried harder, though. Somehow she could have persuaded him to confide in her, and now she had lost the chance for good.

Why should he want to have anything further to do with her and why, she wondered with a surge of longing that pulsed through her body, hadn't she thrown caution and her self-imposed restraint to the winds and allowed her feelings for Alex, matched, she was sure now, by his for her, to have taken them over, there on that secluded beach... ?

It was too late now, though, to have regrets. The Fates would never allow her a second chance.

Dismally, her arms wrapped tightly round her body, Kate crossed the room again and climbed back into bed and though sleep did eventually come it was a restless night she spent, tossing and turning as an insistent and fugitive memory tugged at the edges of her subconscious, something Alex had said which echoed round her brain.

'Don't deny yourself every possibility of happiness.'

The phrase rang round her head, rousing her from sleep when it was still barely light, and she pushed back the bedclothes feeling drained and more tired than when she had gone to bed. Still, once she had packed and began to put the kilometres between her and this ill-fated place she'd forget all about Alex and the disturbing effect he seemed to have on her.

In a short time Kate had showered, packed and tidied up, then a last look round to check she hadn't forgotten anything; it was with a definite sense of release that she finally locked the front door behind her for the very last time.

She'd drop the key in on the caretaker, then...

'So, you really are going this time?'

Kate dropped her cases and spun round, the colour draining from her cheeks.

'Alex? What... where... ?' She stared at him, open-mouthed, her throat suddenly dry with such a plethora of conflicting emotions that she had to reach out to hold on to the car for support.

'Yes, it's me,' Alex replied breezily, 'like the bad penny, or drachma, I've turned up again. I wanted to say goodbye properly.'

'But how did you know when I'd be leaving?' Kate found her voice at last. 'I mean, look, it's only seven o'clock.'

She peered more closely at him, suddenly aware of something odd about his appearance. His clothes were the same, rather more crumpled-looking, maybe, as he'd worn the day before, but his face...

She frowned and Alex's grin widened.

'No, I haven't shaved yet, but I promise you my goodbye kiss will merely brush your cheek in the most decorous way possible. I didn't think this far ahead yesterday or I'd have put a razor in the car.'

'In the car?' Kate echoed weakly, the full implication of all this suddenly sinking in. 'You spent the night *in the car*?'

'That's right. I wanted to make sure I didn't miss you, you see. It was quite comfortable, actually,' he added cheerfully, 'though not quite wide enough to stretch out properly.'

He gave a rueful glance at his long legs which he flexed gingerly, grimacing.

'A bit stiff, but nothing a walk—or swim—won't cure. I suppose,' he went on, with a mischievous sideways grin in her direction, 'you wouldn't think of joining me?'

'For a swim? I don't think so,' Kate replied firmly. 'In any case you said yourself the sea was too cold at this time of year...no thanks.'

'Well, in that case I'll say goodbye, then.' Alex picked up her suitcases which were still where she had dropped them and came over to the car. 'Where do you want these—in the boot?'

Kate nodded and opened it up, watching numbly as he put them carefully in place and shut the lid again.

'So, may I kiss you?'

Again she nodded, gazing wide-eyed up into his face as she waited for his lips to touch her own in farewell and her heart began to thud against her ribs as he rested his hand lightly on her waist to draw her close.

His head came down slowly...slowly...then, only centimetres away from her, it paused. His expression was hidden from her, but she was sure her racing pulses must be giving her away. Why didn't he kiss her and stop tormenting her like this?

She struggled to free herself but the light grasp tightened as Alex straightened up again leaving her unkissed and feeling rather foolish.

'Alex, don't play games with me. If you want to kiss me, do it now and let me leave. I have a long way to go today and I'd planned to be on the road by now.'

Kate brushed aside the thought that this wasn't entirely true. She had in fact no idea where she would be heading but she wasn't going to tell Alex that or he might well try to persuade her to stay after all while she made up her mind.

'I'm not one for wasting my kisses, Miss Penwarden,' he told her gravely. 'So before I do kiss you I have one question to ask, and I want you to think very carefully before you answer me.'

Kate's sigh disguised the lurch her heart gave at his words. 'Very well.'

'Are you, Kate Penwarden, really and truly intending to leave—now, for good?'

'How many times do I have to tell you?' Her impatience was not feigned now. 'Once and for all, Mr Dimitrakos, I am leaving. I have packed, my suitcases are in the car—you put them there yourself—and I have the key to the house here...' She waved it at him in proof. 'As soon as I have given it to the caretaker I shall get into this car and drive away.'

She enunciated these last words very slowly and carefully so that even an idiot would have no difficulty in understanding them, and her eyes began to flash danger signals as she moved to get into the car.

'It's been nice knowing you, as they say. Goodbye, Alex.'

'But I haven't kissed you yet, and as I stayed here all night to do just that you can't refuse me.'

With a couple of swift strides Alex came up behind her, wrapped his arms round her and turned her towards him then, before she could make a single sound of protest, his lips came down on hers. And they weren't as gentle as they had been the evening before, but fierce and demanding as they crushed her mouth with merciless possessiveness.

His jaw rasped against the soft skin of her cheeks and she felt them begin to burn, but not only from their contact with his unshaven chin.

Almost of their own volition her fingers found their way to the crisp curls at the nape of his neck, pulling his head closer to hers with an urgency she could no longer deny, and at the same time his hands abandoned their possession of her waist to move sensuously over her body, easing her shirt from its safe anchorage inside her belted jeans to find the warm, naked flesh beneath.

The muscles deep down in Kate's stomach constricted in a wholly delicious and secret agony as her body melted against his, utterly powerless to withstand the onslaught of emotions and sensations thundering through her and deafening even her own ragged breaths as she gasped for air in the brief intervals between Alex's bruising kisses.

His hands slid round to her midriff, exploring her softness and travelling upwards with tantalising slowness until they reached the taut curves of her aching breasts which he caressed with long, skilful fingers that made them swell against the hard wall of his own chest.

He lifted his head then to gaze, his grey eyes glinting, into Kate's face.

'Do you still want to go, Kate? Can't I persuade you to stay one more day? There's so much I could show you if only you'd let me.'

He stooped to kiss her again, gently this time, brushing his lips across her fiery cheek.

'I'm sorry,' he murmured, not very contritely. 'It must have felt like sandpaper on silk.'

He removed one hand from her breast to touch her face, smoothing it with his thumb, and almost shyly Kate covered it with her own. How could she just walk away from him now, when he'd made her whole body molten with sensations she'd never experienced before? He had made her helpless and he must know it.

'You win,' she said slowly and not quite steadily. 'But I'm not sure you played quite fair.'

'It wasn't a battle,' Alex protested. 'You said you were leaving—in fact, you were quite definite, if you remember. That was just by way of saying goodbye.'

'You have a very odd way of doing it,' Kate observed, painfully conscious that his hand was still cupping her breast, but unsure how to extricate herself from his embrace—or if she wanted to.

'It was my last chance to do something I've been wanting to do ever since I first saw you glaring at me in the airport.'

At last Alex removed his hand from its warm resting-place and thrust both into his pockets as he stepped back to lean against Kate's car, studying her astonished expression with the old familiar humour dancing in his eyes.

'You looked so disapproving when I upset your papers, like some Victorian schoolmarm, all stiff and starchy. I just wanted to make you unbend a little. And I have, haven't I?'

Kate turned away to gaze back at the olive-shaded cottage which seemed fated to be her home for one night longer.

'Yes,' she heard herself saying with a little sigh. 'Yes, you have.'

CHAPTER SEVEN

'SO WHAT are these attractions you've managed to persuade me to change my plans to go and see? I hope they're worth it.'

They had gone back into the cottage and Kate was in the kitchen making coffee for them both when she heard a chuckle behind her.

'I don't think it was the attractions of any place which changed your mind about leaving.'

Kate swung round with a fierce glare that made Alex flinch and put up a hand as though to ward off an imaginary blow.

'Rather ungallant of me, that—I'm sorry,' he said not very apologetically as he propped himself against the doorframe to grin infuriatingly at her. 'I do actually have somewhere in mind, but I think I'll keep it a secret for the moment, just in case you don't like the sound of it after all and change your mind—again.'

He straightened up to walk away into the living-room then paused to add as an afterthought, 'You might bring some sort of swimsuit. My guess is that today will turn out quite hot.'

Kate busied herself with the coffee, not daring to let her mind drift forward to what might lie ahead and not backwards, either, to those devastating moments in Alex's arms, although her still burning cheeks made it impossible for her to forget them altogether.

She concentrated as hard as she could on each little task, making the coffee, serving and drinking it, then washing up the cups with careful deliberation, but all the time nerve-quiveringly conscious of that masculine presence which had so disrupted her life when she had least expected it.

She put the cups away and was staring blankly out of the window, twisting the dishcloth in her hands, when Alex's voice interrupted her unsettled musings.

'Are you ready to go, then? Or do you want to unpack first?'

'Unpack?'

Alex had brought Kate's suitcases back into the cottage, but she hadn't bothered to take them up to her room.

'No, I'll leave those where they are,' Kate declared firmly. 'It's hardly worth unpacking as I shall need them tomorrow. I shall be going then, I promise you. You won't be able to make me change my mind again.'

'Fine, I believe you,' Alex murmured. 'In that case we'd better make the most of today. So, if you've got all you'll need ... ?'

'We'd better make a quick stop at my house, if you don't mind,' he said a short while later as they were driving along the now familiar road between Kate's cottage and his village. 'There are one or two things I need to collect, and I think I ought to shave, don't you?'

He glanced sideways with a glint in his eyes that added an extra flush to Kate's already rosy cheeks, and she muttered something non-committal as she turned away to gaze out of the window at the passing scenery.

Clearly the day wouldn't end without more kisses, and how she would respond to another such onslaught as had almost overwhelmed her earlier that morning she didn't dare speculate. Supposing ... ?

Briefly she shut her eyes. There was no doubt in her mind as to the answer to that unfinished question, and she trembled with sudden trepidation, fearful not of the man beside her but of the strength of her own hidden desires which he seemed to have the power to kindle.

If she was more than usually silent on the short journey to Alex's house he made no comment, and by the time he had returned to the car, shaved and carrying a bag presumably holding his own swimming gear, she had regained most of her shaken composure; but any residual qualms that lingered in the corners of her mind were soon eliminated altogether as Alex turned inland from the coast. The twists and turns of any road Kate had so far travelled on paled into insignificance beside those of the road that had been blasted through the Taygetus mountains from one side of the Mani peninsula to the other, zigzagging its way in a series of steep, acute-angled hairpin bends through thickly wooded gorges where waterfalls plunged down sheer cliff faces beneath towering snow-capped peaks.

Even Alex fell unusually silent as steering the car along this precipitous route took all his concentration and Kate was glad she didn't have to make conversation and reveal the dryness of her mouth. Only when he drew in alongside a little shady café perched by a slight widening in the road did she begin to breathe normally.

'My!' she exclaimed rather shakily. 'That was some journey. Not for the faint-hearted, exactly!'

Alex climbed out and came round to open Kate's door, holding out his hand to help her to her feet.

'It's often impassable in winter,' he told her cheerfully, 'but I thought you ought to see it. Now, what about a restorative coffee before we press on? We haven't got there yet.'

'There', Alex finally informed her as they were driving across the green plain of Sparta, was to be the little port of Yithion.

'It's nothing special, I suppose, but I'm fond of it, and it has some quite interesting associations, too,' he said, slanting an enigmatic smile in her direction. 'Anyway, we'll be there soon and you can tell me what you think.'

There might be nothing particularly remarkable about the small port Alex drove her into a short while later—no ruins or temples—but it did have a charm of its own with its harbour and long sea wall sheltering the fishing and leisure boats moored along the quayside.

'Goodness, whatever are those?' Kate exclaimed, noticing suddenly some strange objects which appeared to be pegged out to dry. To her curious eyes they looked more like dessicated multi-fingered gloves than anything else which sprang to mind.

Alex stopped to have a look. '*Calamares,*' he told her, 'or squid, to you. They catch a lot of them round here, which reminds me...I don't know about you, but I'm starving. We've only had two cups of coffee since our grilled fish last night...and that seems a very long time ago,' he added in a low voice as the hand which had casually been holding hers moved to slide up her bare arm to press her closer to him.

Kate's heart gave a flutter which she tried to ignore. 'Yes, it does seem a long time,' she agreed brightly, 'and I am hungry, now you mention it.'

Leaving his arm where it was, comfortably draped across her shoulders, Alex guided her along to a little taverna overlooking the harbour.

'Ioannis cooks the best *calamares* in Greece—or so he's always telling me, aren't you, my friend?' he smiled at the heavily mustachioed proprietor who came to greet them.

'Of course, Kyrie Alexandros. And today you are in luck. As well as the *calamares* I have my special fish soup—unless your friend would prefer something else? Fresh sardines, perhaps?'

Ioannis fixed dark, fierce eyes on Kate, who was irresistibly reminded of the statue of Black Michael in the square of Areopolis. He seemed to be sizing her up—maybe comparing her mentally with all the other girls Alex had brought here to sample his *calamares*, she thought with a severe pang of jealousy which took her by surprise, but she had no time to let her thoughts dwell on this disturbing discovery as she was led inside the taverna to peer at the dishes on view in Ioannis's kitchen.

'What do you think? Would you like the soup to start with? Of course, there's no choice about what we have for our main course. Ioannis would never speak to me again if we didn't have his *calamares*.'

Tactfully, Kate settled on the soup as a starter, and a Greek salad to accompany the main dish, then they went out into the sunshine again to take their places at the table already prepared for them.

The meal, washed down by another bottle of retsina, was every bit as delicious as both Alex and Ioannis had promised it would be, and by the time they had finished all Kate felt like doing, after the disturbed night she had spent, was having a good long sleep.

'Oh, I am sorry!' she exclaimed, embarrassed at the huge yawn that escaped her. 'Put it down to that large meal and the wine, and the sun, too, after a more or less sleepless night.'

She smiled ruefully at Alex, too contentedly replete to bother to move her hand which suddenly found itself captured by his. Not that she wanted to remove it, it felt warm and strong, and his body, too, would be warm and strong if he were to put his arms round her and hold her close.

She studied him across the table, letting her gaze drift to the grey eyes flecked with gold—or was it green? She'd never really noticed before—and the wide, firm mouth she remembered pressing with bruising intensity to her own...

'Kate? Are you all right?'

'Mmm...' She smiled again, all at once feeling rather dazed, and shook her head to try to clear it.

'I feel fine,' she averred. 'Just a bit sleepy——'

'And maybe just a little... shall we say intoxicated?' Alex suggested, grinning. 'Come on, you can't fall asleep here. We'll go for a little walk, then—well, we'll see.'

He helped her to her feet and they said their goodbyes to Ioannis before setting off down the road with Alex firmly and deliciously supporting her.

'Where are we off to now?' Kate enquired, sensing a purpose in Alex's long strides.

'Not far,' Alex told her, not very informatively, as he glanced back towards the harbour. 'Did you know, the ancient Greeks thought the gods were responsible for building this place? And by the way,' he added totally inconsequentially, 'why couldn't you sleep? Nothing to do with that fish I cooked, I hope?'

Kate shook her head then frowned, finding it difficult after all that had happened since to cast her mind back to her restless state of the previous night. 'It wasn't anything to do with the fish. That was delicious.'

Alex's arm tightened its hold. 'So if it wasn't indigestion...?'

The unspoken question hung between them as Kate struggled to find an answer that would satisfy him without giving too much away. She could hardly confess that it had been thoughts of him that had caused her insomnia.

Finally she gave up. 'It doesn't matter now,' she sighed at last. 'Let's just say uncertainties and regrets of various kinds.'

'And they've gone now?' Alex stopped again and pulled Kate round to face him, placing both hands on her shoulders as he stared deep into her eyes.

'Yes,' he murmured, more to himself than to her. 'I think they have, for the time being. And it's up to me to make sure they don't return, for the rest of today, at least. After that...'

He shrugged and dropped his hands to walk slowly on. 'If you're leaving tomorrow, as you keep insisting you are, I won't be there to keep them at bay, will I?'

Was it Kate's imagination playing tricks, or had there been a touch of bitterness behind his lightly spoken words? She watched the broad back in front of her, trying to find some indication in the set of his shoulders as to what he might really be thinking, but as usual he was giving nothing away and he didn't even seem to expect a reply as he strolled to the side of the road and waited for her to catch him up.

'See that island?' He pointed to a low rocky islet just offshore, and Kate nodded. 'It doesn't look anything out of the ordinary, does it? But there must have been something about it once. Helen of Troy and Paris spent their honeymoon night there.'

He paused, his mouth curved into a gently mocking smile. 'Do you think they—she, anyway—felt regrets and uncertainties as she lay in her lover's arms and remembered the husband she'd left behind?'

'I shouldn't think she'd have given her husband—Menelaus, wasn't it?—a second thought. She was too much in love with Paris, or else she wouldn't have run away with him in the first place, would she?'

There was a long pause before Alex answered her in a low voice Kate could hardly hear, 'No, I guess not.'

The sun was very bright now, but Kate wondered whether it was just its brilliance that made Alex narrow his eyes as he gazed fixedly towards the island, but no sooner had the doubt crossed her mind than she saw his expression lighten again into a wry smile.

'This is hardly the time or the place to embark on a philosophical discussion about love. Come on, let's leave the ghosts to themselves. I think we could both do with a siesta, and I know just the spot.'

He slipped his arm through Kate's and trying to convince herself that the pounding of her heart was merely due to indigestion following a surfeit of *calamares* and nothing to do with anticipation of what might lie ahead, she allowed him to guide her back to the car.

'I hope you think postponing your departure for another day has been worth it so far?' Alex enquired casually as he turned on the engine and prepared to set off on yet another mystery tour.

'I don't know when I've been so lazy, or so spoilt, either,' Kate confessed with a sigh of unfeigned contentment as she settled back for the drive. 'And I can't imagine why you...'

She caught Alex's eye and changed the subject quickly. 'What about your work, though? Shouldn't you be seeing to things at the hotel, or something?'

'Not even "or something",' Alex told her firmly. 'As for spoiling you, as you put it, I could justify that, if spoiling anyone ever needs justification, by saying that I am working, in a way, and doing a PR job on my corner of Greece, so that you'll get all your friends to come and take their holidays here.'

'In your hotel, of course.'

'Of course.'

Kate closed her eyes, lulled by the warmth of the sun on her face and by the soothing motion of the car.

'And they'll all get this VIP treatment, too, will they, being wined and dined and chauffeured about all the beauty spots?'

'Naturally,' came the grave reply. 'This has been by way of being a trial run to see how the itinerary appeals to the discerning tourist.'

'What else could you have possibly have had in mind?' Kate murmured drowsily.

Without even having to lift her heavy eyelids she could see in her mind's eye the quizzical smile curving Alexander's lips.

'What else, indeed, Miss Penwarden? Do you know, if I didn't know you better, I'd think you were flirting?

Not something I'd have expected from an independently minded businesswoman with feminist tendencies such as yourself.'

'Blame the retsina,' Kate heard herself say as though from a long distance, 'or the sun, or...'

Her words trailed off into silence as she fell into a kind of waking doze, barely aware of what was happening or where Alex was taking her, and she was only jolted back into full consciousness by the change in motion as the car bumped suddenly to a halt.

Lazily she opened her eyes and moved her head sideways to find Alex smiling at her.

'Sorry about that,' he said. 'Greek lay-bys don't make for the smoothest of rides—as you have cause to remember.'

Kate struggled into a more upright position and peered out of the window.

'Where are we now? I can't see anything except rocks and more rocks and a few bushes. Are there mythical connections with this place, too?'

'Not so far as I know,' Alex laughed. 'Come on, I'll show you—and this is the moment to bring your swimsuit. Unless you'd prefer to go on dozing here?'

Without waiting for her reply or to see whether she was in fact following him, he strode off down a narrow path almost invisible between the rocks, leaving Kate to scramble after him and pick her way gingerly over the stones until she found herself at the bottom of the cliff where Alexander was waiting to lift her off the final boulder on to the silvery sand of yet another tiny, deserted cove.

Kate stared round in delight, trying to ignore the fact that Alex was still holding her.

'What a lovely spot!' she exclaimed, before turning to him with wide, innocent eyes. 'How many of these little beaches do you know? Do you have one for every day of the week?'

'At least,' Alex informed her gravely. 'And one for each of my many girlfriends. That way none of them gets jealous. But this one is reserved for very special people—and special occasions,' he added softly, slipping his arm further round her waist and leading her to the water's edge.

'This is the place I told you about where the water's always warm, and, although it might not be quite so inaccessible as the other beach, not many people find that path. We should have it all to ourselves—and, besides, there's only room for two.'

A glance round confirmed the accuracy of Alex's statement, and Kate's pulses quickened at the huskiness that had crept into his voice. She was in his hands, the strong, brown hands now enclosing her own, and there was little if any chance of making an escape from this rocky shore. It seemed that the Fates had, after all, given her a second chance—if she wanted to take it.

She turned her back on the sparkling turquoise sea to gaze inland at the massive cliffs towering above them, from which had tumbled great boulders which now littered the beach as though hurled there by some giant child in a fit of temper.

Without relinquishing his possessive grasp of her fingers Alex led the way back up the beach to the rug he had dropped at the foot of the rocks and pulled her down beside him. Kate leaned her head back and closed her eyes, feeling the breeze caress her skin, still tender from Alex's unshaven kisses earlier that day, and she smiled, knowing he was looking at her and relishing the knowledge.

'It's so peaceful here,' she murmured drowsily.

'And you're so beautiful.'

She felt him move beside her, sensing his breath on her face before his lips touched her. His fingers lightly stroked her cheek.

'Still sore?'

'Mmm—just a bit.'

Kate opened her eyes, which widened in instinctive response as his mouth pressed more urgently to hers, and his fingers moved from her face to slide down the curve of her throat . . . her neck . . . to come to rest on her uptilted breast.

Kate dared not move as through her veins ran the most rapturous fear that even the slightest tremor might be enough to make him remove his hand, which with infinitesimal caresses was arousing such unendurably delicious sensations through her whole body.

Just as she felt she could endure the agony of anticipation no longer, Alex leapt to his feet with shocking suddenness to stand over her, raking her with narrowed, glittering eyes that almost frightened her by the intensity of their gaze.

What had she done wrong? Nothing that she could think of.

'Alex, what . . . ?' She sat up and hugged her knees as she stared at him in hurt perplexity. 'Is there something the matter? Something I've done?'

Her words drifted miserably away as he shook his head impatiently.

'Nothing.' There was a new harshness in his voice as he continued to gaze down at her and she saw his hands clench into tight fists by his sides. 'You've done nothing. How could you have, lying back there so soft and so lovely, like a peach ripe for the plucking? So how could I trust myself?'

He swung round and began tearing off his clothes. 'I'm going for a swim before I do something you—and I—might regret.'

Kate bit back the words of protest as she saw his shirt drop to the ground, followed by his jeans, revealing his strong, broad torso permanently tanned by many a hot summer sun, and as she watched him, fascinated, an urge she could hardly contain swept over her to feel that fit, hard body pressed once more to her own softer curves.

But Alex ignored her totally as with a final, almost savage gesture he flung his shoes away and ran down to the sea, to plunge in and cleave his way through the water with the long, smooth strokes of an experienced and powerful swimmer.

Kate's eyes fell on the bag that contained her own swimming things. This wasn't the time to join Alex for a light-hearted bathe. By his own admission he needed time to cool off, in more senses than one before...before what?

What *would* happen when he came back to join her? Would he have regained his normal self-possession, or would he find it impossible to restrain himself from taking advantage of the privacy of this little beach—and of her? If he really cared to, he could overpower her utterly here. There was nowhere she could run to, no one to hear any cries for help.

Slowly Kate got to her feet and almost unthinkingly went to pick up Alex's scattered clothing, lifting his shirt briefly to her face to inhale the faintly musky, totally masculine scent of his body, and in that moment she knew, in a blaze of recognition almost dizzying in its violence, that his lightest touch, the softest kiss, would deliver her to his desire totally and willingly.

She slipped off her own shoes and rolled up her jeans, then walked to the water's edge. Tiny wavelets lapped at the gritty white sand under her toes, the sparkling water just as warm as Alex had told her it would be. Almost warm enough to tempt her in...

Alex had turned now and was swimming back towards her, slowly, as though his tension had been washed away in the blue depths of the sea, and he waved cheerfully at her.

'Come on in,' he shouted. 'It really is warm, I promise you.'

Kate gave a tentative wave back as he dived beneath the surface, to re-emerge only yards away, his brown, wet body glistening in the sun.

'Come on,' he urged her again. 'I'll wait for you. You'll be sorry if you don't give it a try. And I'll turn my back while you change—no peeping, honestly.'

'It's not that,' Kate protested, meeting his teasing gaze doubtfully. Could she have mistaken his earlier mood? Had it not been suppressed desire for her that had driven him away so precipitately, but some other emotion she couldn't even guess at? It was difficult to judge, when most of the time he gave the impression of taking life very much as it came—people, too.

'Well?' Alex persisted, splashing water over his shoulders before ducking down again. 'If you're not going to join me, I'll go for another swim. I'm getting cold waiting for you to make your mind up.'

'Hang on, I won't be a minute.'

Kate ran up the beach. There was no turning back now, whatever the consequences. She pulled her shirt out of her jeans and began undoing the buttons, unable to prevent herself from glancing back over her shoulder to check whether Alex was holding to his promise.

She grinned as she saw his back resolutely turned towards her. She ought to have known him well enough to realise he wouldn't cheat.

'Right, here I am,' she heard herself saying in a strangely tight voice. 'You can turn round now.'

She dropped the towel she was carrying on a patch of shingle and swished through the shallow water to join him.

'My!' There was an unmistakable gleam of hunger in the grey eyes that slid over her body, and Kate knew it wasn't just the sea breeze brushing her bare skin that turned it briefly to gooseflesh.

'That was worth waiting for,' Alex said softly as his gaze travelled slowly down each inch of her body, lin-

gering on the swell of her breasts moulded to ripe curves
by the clinging peacock-blue material of her swimsuit,
over the contours of her stomach which contracted as
though at a physical caress, to her bare legs and then
back with equal deliberation until they reached her face
once more.

Kate felt her heart begin to race, sure his sharp eyes
could find the uneven pulses beneath their skin-tight
covering, and a shudder ran through her as his cold, wet
hand reached for hers.

'Come on,' he ordered her hoarsely. 'I'll race you to
that rock. Or do you need a head start?'

Kate gave him a brief glare before wrenching her hand
free to dive forward, gasping as the cool water enveloped her.

She swam with long, even strokes towards the rock
Alex had indicated, knowing she had no chance of
beating him to it, but grateful for the opportunity of
having something else to concentrate on and letting her
churned-up emotions settle down to something like their
normal state—whatever that was, she thought wryly. She
had no illusions now about the nature of Alex's feelings
for her, nor, if she was strictly honest, of her own for
him. What to do about them was something she couldn't
begin to fathom, not here—not now.

Alex came up beside her and matched her slower
strokes with his own.

'No regrets? It is warm, isn't it?'

'Lovely.' Kate turned on to her back to float, arms
stretched out sideways, and stared up at the clear blue
sky. 'And no, no regrets.'

She glanced towards him, feeling her hair spread out
round her head. 'And you don't have to keep asking me
that, you know. Whatever it was that kept me awake
last night has no place here. In fact,' she added slowly
as she kicked out to propel her alongside him, 'I'm not
even sure I can remember what it was all about now.'

Alex put in a couple of strokes that brought him to the rock they had been heading for and clambered out, reaching down to pull Kate up beside him on to its flat top.

'It's not very big, is it?' Kate commented with a suddenly constricted throat as Alex's arm went round her to hold her against him.

'Just big enough,' he replied cheerfully. 'And don't fall off, the sea's much colder that side. There's a freshwater spring down there where the water's eddying.'

'There's not much chance of my doing that, is there?' Kate observed drily, painfully conscious of the proximity of their two wet bodies, of their thighs, Alex's hard and brown with its covering of dense black hair and her own, smooth and pale, pressed to it.

With his free hand Alex pushed the heavy locks of wet hair back from her face and leant over to kiss her cheek.

'They say mermaids have been seen lying on this rock, luring sailors—and swimmers too, I daresay—to their fate,' he murmured against her ear as the hand holding her tightened its pressure on her waist. 'But until this moment I've never believed it. And now I've captured one—a sea-green woman all of my own.'

Alex's lips moved from her cheek to Kate's shoulder, nudging the thin strap of her swimsuit towards the top of her arm—and danger. 'If you kiss a mermaid, will she turn mortal again, I wonder? Prickly and independent, and full of the regrets I'm not supposed to mention?'

Kate's heart was pounding so hard now that she knew Alex must be able to feel it shaking her body.

'You'll have to risk it,' she said unsteadily. 'You won't know till you try.'

Powerless now to resist the desire that had been simmering deep within her ever since—when? Their first meeting? She didn't know, and it didn't matter—she tilted her head back against his hard, bronzed shoulder and offered her lips for the kiss she knew would seal her captivity finally.

'You taste nice,' Alex said softly as he smiled into her eyes. He ran his tongue over her mouth, parting her lips as though savouring her unique flavour, she thought dazedly.

'So do you.' Her voice was hardly more than a whisper, muffled by his own kisses, and suddenly, unable to bear the ecstasy any longer, she turned and buried her face against his chest.

There was a quick intake of breath and Kate could feel Alex's heart leap as his arms tightened round her to hold her close in a fierce yet magically tender embrace.

If only it could last for ever, this enchantment woven round them by sun and sea, this warm closeness of their two bodies. If only they could stay here for eternity in this private, timeless paradise... but even as the longing swept through her she felt Alex move to slip his hands beneath her chin and tilt her face towards his.

'Come, mermaid.'

He slid into the water, holding out his arms to Kate who fell into them with a gasp, but it was not only the chill of the cold waters lapping round her body that made her shudder in the strong embrace that propelled her slowly towards the shore. There was an unmistakable purpose now in all Alex's movements and a hunger in the eyes devouring her, their gaze as fathomless as the sea itself. It would be as easy to drown in one as in the other, Kate thought wildly, realising she had lost the power, even the will, to resist either man or element as she was borne relentlessly along in Alex's arms.

The water was waist high when he stopped to hold her away from him, to rake her slowly with eyes whose predatory gleam left her in no doubt of how much he wanted her.

'You are so beautiful,' he said slowly, drawing her closer to enfold her tightly in his arms.

Kate felt her body melt against his, rejoicing shamelessly in the thrust of male desire against her, and with a low moan she buried her face against his wet chest in an instinctive but useless urge to hide the flame of passion raging in her blood, only too visible on her suffused cheeks.

Alex laughed, a soft, rasping sound that caused a shiver to run up her backbone.

'You want me, don't you, mermaid? There's no use denying it. Maybe you should have taken your chance to escape this morning, but it's too late now. Your spell has worked its magic too well.'

He scooped her up in his arms and waded through the water, carrying her as easily as he might have a child, to deposit her gently on the warm sand where she lay motionless and gazing up at him with wide, expectant eyes.

He stood over her for a moment, silhouetted black against the brightness of the sky, until unhurriedly and with great deliberation he lowered himself beside her, his eyes narrowing as they travelled slowly down the length of her body and back.

Gone now was the humorous light in his eyes which for an instant glittered cold as an eagle's as he scooped her up in one strong arm, holding her against his chest as the other hand pushed away the peacock-blue shoulder straps and thrust them down her arms to uncover her nakedness.

With a kind of groan he buried his face in the soft valley between the swell of her breasts, then lifted his head to cup first one then the other with long, hard fingers that seemed to tremble as they touched her damp skin.

Kate's whole body ached, yielding itself up to the agonising sensuousness of his caresses, and she arched against him, hardly aware, in her state of total abandon, of the hand that was now easing her swimsuit down...down, over her hipbones, down her thighs, until with a cry of primeval triumph Alex flung it away on to the sand, rolling over to kneel astride her, his eyes shining with the light of conquest.

'You can't escape now,' he taunted her, 'not even if you wanted to—but you don't, do you?'

She lifted her arms to twine them round his neck, drawing his head down to her own with an answering smile of feminine compliance as old as time itself.

'No, Alex,' she murmured, her lips moving with difficulty, crushed as they were beneath his own. 'I want to stay here, with you, for ever and ever...'

What had happened to all her so-called old-fashioned morality, as Michael had mockingly called it, to say nothing of her cherished independence of spirit, and her determination to go it alone for the rest of her life without any further involvement with men—any man?

Alex was what—who—had happened, first with his undemanding kindness, then with his persistence and the overwhelming urgency with which he was battering at her pathetic defences.

She groaned, her eyes closed, as waves of agonising delight bore her along on a flood of sensuality with each skilful caress and every kiss that seemed to draw up the very essence of her being to answer the insistent demands of his hands and mouth.

There was no doubt about the force of his desire for her, his body hard and uncompromisingly male as he pressed her to the ground, summoning up her response until her whole being seemed to be on fire, matching the heat of the sun itself as it blazed down on them, blinding in its intensity. Then, as her cry echoed from all the surrounding rocks, the sky itself seemed to split in half, and everything went black...

'My darling...'

Strange, Kate thought dazedly as Alex's soft voice woke her from her blissful coma, the sun's still there, up in the sky, shining down on the two of us as though nothing had happened, and yet...

'Kate?'

She turned then within the circle of his arms to find him smiling into her face with a tenderness unlike any she had seen before, not even in her dreams.

'Where were you?'

'Up there—lost, somewhere in infinity.' She waved a hand vaguely towards the blue, sunlit expanses above them before resting it on his cheek. 'It's funny, the sky's blue again. It went quite dark just now.'

Alex's head moved just enough for him to be able to touch her lips with his. 'It was the gods,' he said gravely. 'They stole the sun so they couldn't see us. They were jealous, you see.'

His arms tightened round her to draw her close again and he covered her with kisses so light that they felt like the caress of a breeze wafting in from the sea.

There was no need for words. Their lips and hands and the closeness of their bodies were more than enough to express it all—the passion and the magic of what had just happened, Kate thought in wonder. It was all so extraordinary and so very, very marvellous.

'Why are you smiling?' Alex traced the line of her mouth with his finger before stooping to brush it again with his own.

'I didn't know I was,' Kate replied with a sigh that seemed to well up from the very depths of her being. 'Probably because I'm utterly, completely happy.'

Alex disengaged one arm from behind her head to prop himself up on his elbow and gaze down into her face, smiling himself.

'You are also very sandy,' he observed, 'and shameless with it. You do know, of course, that Greeks disapprove very strongly of nude sunbathing? I'm surprised the tourist police haven't arrived by now.'

'They haven't, though, have they?' Kate enquired lazily, making no effort to cover herself. She moved sensuously in the warm sand, taunting him with her eyes. 'But you're a Greek, Kyrie Alexandros Dimitrakos—or half of you is. Do you disapprove too? I'm sorry if I've offended you. There were mitigating circumstances, though, and I was rather led astray. In fact——'

'Siren.'

Kate was prevented from saying anything more in her self-defence as Alex flung himself, spread-eagled, across her, to crush the breath from her lungs and punish her mouth with hard, merciless kisses that left her bruised and gasping when at last he lifted his head from hers.

'That's the punishment meted out for impertinence.'

'And nude sunbathing?' Kate enquired rather shakily.

'That too.' Alex knelt up by her supine body, placing his two hands on either side of her head to gaze down into her face.

'This wasn't planned, you know, when I asked you to stay on today. At least, not entirely.' A smile flickered momentarily at the corners of his lips. 'But I have no regrets about how things turned out. And I hope you haven't?'

Their eyes, the grey and the green, met and held, and Kate moved her head with a gesture of utter contentment as she smiled her answer back at him.

'No,' she whispered, reaching up to cover his hands with hers. 'None at all.'

CHAPTER EIGHT

THEY did not speak much on the journey back to Kate's cottage, and Kate lay back in her seat in a state of total bliss, just letting her mind wander where the fancy took it, thinking back to the beginning of the day when she'd found Alex waiting for her, to Yithion where Helen of Troy had honeymooned with her lover and on to that enchanted cove. She turned and smiled at *her* lover.

'We're not on the same road as this morning, surely?' she asked with a desultory glance through the window at the passing fields and orchards. There wasn't a hairpin to be seen anywhere.

Alex shook his head. 'I thought a more restful route would be more appropriate after...' He rested his hand on Kate's thigh, his mere touch enough to summon up a surge of desire that contracted the muscles in her stomach and she heard a little laugh as he withdrew his hand to negotiate a bend in the road, but although he made no comment Kate knew he'd sensed the emotions his caress had aroused in her only too susceptible body.

And where was all this going to lead? Kate closed her eyes as though to blot the question from her mind, but it refused to go away. What was going to happen when they got back to the cottage—and what would she do tomorrow? Would she—could she—put this day, and Alex, resolutely behind her once and for all and leave as though nothing had happened? As she had kept insisting she would?

Alex had promised not to try to dissuade her again. Would he keep his promise, and, if he did, wouldn't she be desperately hurt?

All these questions pounded in her head, threatening to erase from her memory those moments of rapture on the beach which the unwelcome voice of common sense was even now trying to persuade her had meant nothing but 'dalliance' to the man by her side.

He hadn't told her any differently, and she certainly wasn't going to ask him. She had her pride still.

And what had they meant to her? Kate sneaked a sideways glance at the tall, relaxed figure beside her, meeting his quick smile with a rather uncertain one of her own. That was something she could hardly dare contemplate, not while he was here, so close, and able to arouse sensations in her that she had never imagined it possible for anyone to experience.

She tried to think of more mundane matters, such as the opening of her new boutique, and whether Liz was coping on her own, but somehow all that seemed impossibly remote and, strangely, not terribly important. The present, and Alex, and the truth of their feelings for one another, were what mattered.

'I would invite you for a meal,' she ventured prosaically when they had rejoined the coast road and were heading for home, 'but there's no food in the cottage. I was preparing to move out this morning, if you remember?'

She tried to inject a convincing note of light-heartedness into her voice, and Alex grinned.

'I do seem to recall some such notion. I wonder what made you change your mind.'

He met Kate's glare with equanimity. 'As for the meal, I was hoping you'd let me take you out. It is your last evening here, after all.'

If Kate was disappointed at the matter-of-fact way in which he made this last comment she had only herself to blame, she reminded herself sternly, with her constantly stressed determination to move on, so why should Alex continue any longer in his efforts to dissuade her?

'Well?'

'Sorry. I was miles away.' Kate refocused her eyes on his and smiled ruefully. 'I don't see why you should take me out again. After all, you've already treated me to one meal today. Couldn't I treat you instead?'

'Out of the question,' Alex told her firmly. 'As a Greek—or as a Scot—I couldn't possibly accept—thanks all the same. However,' he added, swinging the car round to drive up the track to Kate's temporary home, 'there is one thing you could do for me, before we go out.'

'Of course,' Kate replied, with a slight constriction in her throat at the thought of what he might be going to ask her.

'What I need more than anything,' he told her airily though with just the suspicion of a grin as though he knew only too well what she was thinking, 'is a shower. Somehow—I can't imagine how—I seem to have got covered with sand. It could be that you are too?'

He brought the car to a halt outside her front door and leant across to open the passenger door, but his hand stopped on the way to brush her cheek.

'That was quite a day,' he murmured. 'One to remember, for me, anyway.'

His hand slipped down to cup her chin and tilt her head back to receive the kiss he dropped on her lips.

'What about you, Kate? Will you remember it as you take off for new horizons?'

He looked long and hard into her eyes as he waited for her reply which, when it came, was scarcely more than a whisper.

'I'll remember.'

He kissed her again, full on her mouth, but gently and with none of the passion they had shared on the enchanted beach, then he stretched over and opened her door.

'So, what about that shower?'

                    *   *   *

It was while Kate was in the bathroom that there was a knock at the front door.

Alex had had his shower first and was dressing in the spare bedroom. 'I'll go, shall I? Are you expecting anyone?' he called out to Kate through the bathroom door.

He heard the water being turned off and moments later a dripping face peered at him round the corner of the door.

'Sorry, I couldn't hear. What did you say?'

The unknown visitor knocked again, more insistently, and Kate frowned.

'Whoever can that be? What a time to call!'

'They seem very keen to see you, whoever it is. Would you like me to go and answer the door for you? You can hardly go like that.'

He pointed at the towel Kate was clutching to her, one eyebrow lifting in gentle mockery.

'Hardly necessary, all that modesty, is it, when you think what I've already...?' He let the sentence drift away, but his meaning was all too clear as was the teasing glint in his eyes.

Kate glared at him and held the towel more tightly. 'That was different.'

'Mmm—I'll agree there. It was, very different, and very nice—just the two of us beneath the sun, on the sand——'

'—which I'm now trying to wash out of my hair,' Kate reminded him firmly, 'and I would be very grateful if you could answer the door. Tell whoever it is I'll be down in a minute or two when I've made myself decent.'

As Alex opened the front door he saw the expression on the tall stranger's face change from one of expectancy to a doubtful frown.

'Can I help you?' Alex enquired, assuming at first sight that the man was Greek, and speaking in his native tongue. 'Are you lost, or looking for someone?'

The man looked even more uncertain and gave Alex a rueful smile. 'Do you speak English?' he asked slowly. 'I'm afraid I do not know any Greek.'

Alex gave a quick glance at the third car parked outside and noticed the hire company's sticker on the windscreen. 'Not many tourists do,' he said pleasantly, smiling at the relief on the other man's face as he heard words spoken fluently in his own language.

'I'm sorry to have troubled you,' he told Alex. 'I must have been misdirected. I'm really looking for an English girl who's staying somewhere around her, a Miss Kate Penwarden, but I must have got it wrong.'

'I see.' A shadow crossed Alex's face, but if the stranger saw it he was unaware of its cause. 'No,' he went on slowly, 'you haven't got it wrong. This is where she's staying.'

He turned and went inside, leaving the other man to decide whether or not to follow him, and climbed halfway up the stairs.

'Kate?' he called out, his voice oddly harsh. 'I think you'd better come down. You have a visitor.'

There was a short pause, then Kate emerged from the bathroom clad in a wrap, her feet bare and with a towel wrapped turban-wise round her head.

'A visitor, did you say? For me? But who…? Michael!'

Alex saw her eyes widen briefly before she swayed, her face deathly pale as she clutched the banisters for support, and he ran up to take her arm, ignoring the astonished stare of the other man.

'Come on,' he said quietly. 'You'd better come down.'

Kate hardly seemed to be aware of what was happening as Alex led her slowly down to the living-room and sat her down in a chair. Her eyes were fixed, staring with shock at the face of the man who until only a few short weeks ago had been her fiancé and who had followed her out to Greece. But why?

'Michael,' she repeated in a dull voice. 'What are you doing here?'

'I might ask you the same question,' Michael said grimly, glancing from Kate to Alex whose arm was still protectively round her shoulders. 'Aren't you going to introduce me to your friend?'

'Oh—yes.' Ignoring the sneering note in Michael's voice, Kate ran her hands wearily over her face. 'Michael, this is Alexandros Dimitrakos. We met on the plane and he has been very kind, he and his sister,' she added firmly as she began to try to get a grip of the situation. 'I had a slight accident when I arrived, and they looked after me for a day or two. Today he's been showing me round.'

'But you're better now, I hope?' Michael enquired with icy politeness. 'Well enough to enjoy your sightseeing?' His eyes ran over her body and Kate pulled her robe more closely round her, knowing her state of nudity beneath must be only too obvious.

'I was having a shower when you arrived,' she explained, and immediately wished she'd kept silent. What business was it of Michael's what she did, or whom she did it with, for that matter? 'You still haven't told me why you've come—there's nothing wrong, is there, no crisis to do with the business?'

She turned to Alex. 'Michael looks after the accounts,' she explained briefly, the thought flashing through her mind even as she spoke that she'd have to find someone else to do that job. The present arrangement would be impossible in the new circumstances.

Michael shook his head. 'No, there's nothing wrong with the business, not as far as I know. I'm here to deal with a purely personal matter.'

Kate's stomach lurched, and she felt Alex's fingers tighten protectively on her shoulder but she dared not look up at him. Instead, she kept her eyes fixed firmly on her knees and clutched the edges of her towelling wrap, her knuckles showing white with tension as she wondered feverishly what was expected of her. For almost the first time in her life she was assailed by a feeling of inadequacy in this wholly unwelcome situation.

A drop of water from her wet hair escaped from under her turban and ran down her forehead, reminding her of what she was supposed to be doing, and she got slowly to her feet and looked helplessly from one man to the other.

'If you'll excuse me, I'll go and get dressed. You did catch me at rather an awkward moment,' she said to Michael with a minute smile that met no response other than a steely glare as he came close to loom over her, but without any attempt to touch her.

'We need to talk,' he said in a low, harsh voice. 'I haven't come all this way for an evening of small talk. Could we have a meal together? Here, for preference. What I have to say is private.'

His cold eyes flicked towards Alex who was standing motionless by the chair Kate had left, watching this interchange with grim curiosity.

'Alex and I are going out,' Kate protested. 'I'm leaving tomorrow, and it was to be a farewell meal. Can't you stay the night in a hotel somewhere and come back in the morning?'

A bleak look touched Alex's face as he turned abruptly away to go and stare out of the window. He thrust his hands deep into his pockets. 'That's all right, Kate. Michael's come a long way to see you. We can say our goodbyes now—if you'll still be leaving?'

Kate gazed miserably at the taut lines of his back, feeling the web of misunderstanding already beginning to trap all three of them, but powerless to break its sticky strands.

'I expect so. Alex, I'm so sorry——' She took a step towards him and he wheeled round to fix her face with a stare of such intensity that she caught her breath as he reached for her hand to hold it just for the briefest of moments.

'A day to remember, Kate,' he said in a low voice meant only for her ears. 'And no regrets.'

He glanced quickly over to the other man whose face was a study in suspicion and mistrust. 'I won't stand in your way.'

Then, before she had time to speak, he was away through the open door, hurrying back to his car.

'Alex ...' Kate ran to the door, but it was already too late. She watched his car reverse, spattering stones and dust behind it, then speed off down the track as though he couldn't wait to make his escape.

What were his final words? 'I won't stand in your way.' Did he really imagine, after all she had told him about her relationship with Michael, that she would even contemplate going back to him?

He couldn't think that, surely, not after all that had happened this afternoon?

Oblivious now to Michael's watchful presence, she stood without moving, her arms wrapped round her body as though to embrace the memory of their lovemaking, staring unseeing at the gnarled branches of the surrounding olive trees as she saw again in her mind's eye the shimmering sea and their two bodies entwined beneath the sun.

'Kate?'

Michael's peremptory voice summoned her back to the present and she walked with slow, reluctant steps back into the house.

'Kate, come in. You can't go standing there like that—it's not decent! Go and get dressed, we need to talk.'

He crossed the room in a couple of long strides and took her hands in his. 'I've come a long way to find you ... as your—friend—pointed out.'

There was an ironic pause after the word 'friend' but Kate let it go unchallenged. This was not the moment to embark on lengthy explanations of her relationship with Alex, and she wasn't even sure she could explain it to herself, she thought sadly as she went upstairs to dry her hair and get dressed.

'I'm sorry, I haven't any food in the house,' she called down. 'I told you I was planning to move on tomorrow, so we'll have to eat out somewhere.'

Not that she had much of an appetite, but it would be a lot easier to have this talk Michael so badly wanted on neutral ground, rather than in the solitary confinement of this small cottage.

'So why are you leaving here so soon?' Michael asked her on her reappearance. Clearly he'd been brooding on this piece of information all the time she had been upstairs. 'Liz told me you'd be here for a fortnight at least. How would I have found you if you'd taken off into the blue?' he ended irritably.

Kate sighed. 'How could I know you'd come looking for me? It certainly wasn't something I expected—or wanted,' she muttered, not quite inaudibly. 'And as for my reasons for wanting to leave here...' She shrugged and turned away to pick up her bag. 'I felt like exploring some more of the country. Nothing wrong in that, is there? Silly not to take advantage of an opportunity like this, and goodness knows when I'll get another holiday, once the second shop's up and running.'

'So it's nothing to do with that fellow—Alexander? You're not going away with him?'

'If I were, that would be my own business, Michael,' Kate told him steadily. 'But if it's any comfort to you, no, I'm not going away with him.'

Michael's tight features eased a fraction as he followed her out of the house, but he did not pursue the point. Plenty of time for that later, he told himself.

'We'll go in my car,' Kate said. 'It'll be easier if I drive—I know the way—and I know you're not all that keen on Greek food, but I'm afraid it's Hobson's choice round here, not unnaturally.'

'If you remember that much about me it's a start, I suppose,' Michael replied, unable to suppress a tinge of bitterness in his voice. 'Actually, though, I'm so hungry I could eat anything. The last meal I had was a sort of breakfast on the plane. I was so anxious to make sure of finding you I didn't dare stop off on the way.'

These words struck a kind of dread into Kate's heart. The last thing she wanted was another confrontation with this man, or to reawaken old emotions, but if he had taken so much trouble to come and see her—for whatever reason—the least she could do was hear him out when the time came. For the moment she must keep the atmosphere between them as light and uncomplicated as she could—not easy when all she wanted to do was to find Alex and discover the meaning behind his parting words.

They drove in silence down to the village and conversation throughout the meal was stilted, as though the two of them were strangers who had only just met, Kate thought bleakly, watching her former fiancé crumble a piece of bread between his fingers as he stared over her head at the darkening sky.

'It's quite attractive, I suppose, in its way—this village, I mean,' he said brusquely. 'But it's a bit quiet, isn't it? Not a lot going on.'

'That's why I came,' Kate pointed out. 'I needed to be somewhere peaceful, on my own, to sort things out in my own mind, after...after everything that had happened.'

'And are you?' Michael enquired drily with a sardonic lift of his eyebrow. 'On your own, that is. In my admittedly rather limited experience it wasn't exactly one of your habits to wander about your house only half dressed in front of comparative strangers.'

Kate drained her glass and screwed up her napkin which she placed with great deliberation on her plate.

'If you're going to keep making snide accusations I shall leave now, Michael. I told you, Alex is a friend, nothing more.'

As she spoke she felt the very words stab arrows of guilt into her heart. Of course Alex wasn't just a friend, and even to say so was a betrayal of him and of all they had shared that magical afternoon, but the precise nature of their relationship she knew she must keep to herself. It was too precious to share, especially with this man, of all people.

She fixed him with a steady gaze. 'We'd been swimming and I was having a shower before we went out for a meal. That's all there was to it,' she continued firmly, 'but if you don't believe me . . . ?'

She made as though to push her chair back but Michael reached out to grasp her wrist.

'No, I'm sorry, Kate. I shouldn't have said that. As you say, what you do now is no business of mine.'

He released her arm and slumped back in his chair, his face suddenly drawn and tired, and Kate couldn't suppress a faint pang of pity for this man she'd once, not so long ago, thought she loved enough to marry.

But all that was over and done with. Michael himself had seen to that, and there was no point in prolonging this painful interview any longer than was absolutely necessary.

'So what did you come all this way to say to me?' she asked resignedly. 'It must be very important.'

'Of course it is,' Michael rasped out so loudly the people at the next table turned and stared. 'I know I behaved like a fool—and worse than a fool,' he went on in a lower tone, fixing her with a bright, hard gaze, then he broke off suddenly.

'Look—can't we go for a walk or something, if we've finished? It's difficult talking with all these people round us.'

Kate glanced round at the diners at nearby tables and grinned in spite of the seriousness of the occasion.

'I don't think you need worry, actually. They're all Greek. There are hardly any tourists about at the moment. Still, if you'd feel more comfortable, we can walk along the harbour.' She got up and led the way outside. 'You can get a good view of the village from there, with the mountains behind. It looks pretty at night.'

'Dammit, Kate, I haven't come all this way to look at the view,' Michael exploded, lengthening his stride to come to stand in front of her, blocking the way. 'You know why I'm here. What happened between Carol and me, it was a thing of the moment, a mistake.'

Kate stared at him, appalled. 'And the baby, Michael? Is that just "a thing of the moment"? A mistake, maybe, but you can't just dismiss it as something of no importance. It's a human being you're talking about!'

'No, it isn't.' Michael gave a harsh laugh. 'That was a mistake, too. A false alarm—whatever.'

'I see.'

'I don't think you do, Kate. I've come to apologise, truly and from the bottom of my heart. I know how much I must have hurt you, but, as I said, it was only a brief affair, for both of us. I swear it. Something got into me I couldn't control, because I wanted you so much.'

He grasped her arms and held them tightly. 'I still want you, more than anything. What we felt for one another can't have vanished—you must still love me, deep down, even though you won't admit it. I'll give you all the time you want to think about it, as long as you come back to me, please. Here, I've brought your ring.'

He released her to fumble in his pocket and brought out a jeweller's box which he tried to thrust into her hand.

'Put it back where it belongs. Your finger looks so bare without it.'

He lifted her left hand and raised it tentatively to his lips which felt hot and feverish, but Kate pulled away as though her skin had been burnt.

'How could you, Michael? How could you even think things could ever be the same, after what you did—and said? About my not being normal for not wanting children,' she flung at him hoarsely. 'That was what hurt most, even more than your affair with Carol—even more than the baby. And I didn't know then that it was only a false alarm, did I? You knew, you've always known, why I decided I couldn't have children—and yet you said *that*.'

Her voice rose as she relived the anguish of their last meeting, and as Michael reached out a hand she swung away from him, hardening her heart against the new, pleading note in his voice.

'I know, Kate, and I could have bitten my tongue out afterwards. The last thing I wanted to do was to hurt you; you should have known that. I just thought, in time... But I can live without children,' he went on softly. 'Lots of people have to, but I can't live without you.'

He came up close behind her and she felt his breath on the back of her neck as he wrapped his arms round her.

'Come back with me,' he murmured, brushing her hair with his lips. 'Or stay on and finish your holiday, if that's what you want, but say something, give me some hope that you will be my wife, one day. I love you, Kate, and I need you.'

He turned her rigid body in his arms and tried to pull her against him, but Kate only felt nauseated by his proximity and thrust him away from her with a desperate longing to feel another man's round her, other lips touching hers.

'It's no use, Michael,' she said steadily. 'It'd never work out, not now, not however long you gave me to think it over.'

'You don't know that,' Michael persisted. 'Just give it—me—another chance. I promise nothing like that will ever happen again, and I need to know at least if there's any hope of us getting together again. That's why I had to come.'

A small suspicion began to niggle deep in Kate's subconscious. She tried to suppress it but there was something about the urgency in Michael's voice, that particular way he had of narrowing his eyes when he was involved in a complicated business deal that made her suddenly uneasy.

'Michael,' she said slowly, 'tell me one thing, and I want an honest answer.'

Michael turned, his eyes not quite able to meet the intensity of her own gaze, and in that instant she knew all she needed to know.

'There's something else connected with your coming here, isn't there? It's not only that you've been pining away without me. There's some pressing reason why you need to know whether I'll change my mind and marry you.'

'Kate, let me explain . . .'

He reached out to touch her but she flung his hands away as though they repelled her.

'How could you?' she burst out. 'How could you use me, making me think you really loved and wanted me, when all the time you had an ulterior motive for asking for a second chance? Heavens, how gullible you must think me!'

She walked away and sat down on a bollard, hunched against the icy chill of her emotions.

'Of course I don't,' Michael protested, following her. 'But I thought maybe a new start, in a different country...'

'Different country?' Kate stared at him in astonishment. 'Michael, what are you talking about?'

'I came here to ask if you'd come with me to Tokyo.'

'I see,' she said in a flat, dull voice.

'No, you don't.' He came nearer to crouch down beside her and stare up into her face, willing her to listen. 'I've been offered a promotion, to head a new office in Tokyo, but——' He paused, trying to frame the sentence as tactfully as he could, but Kate was too quick for him.

'But they want a married man for the job. That's it, isn't it?'

'I wouldn't have put it as crudely as that.'

'It's what it amounts to, though. You want to marry me so you can get a better job.'

'For both of us,' Michael insisted. 'It would be a great chance for both of us. A new start, in a different place. Think of it, Kate—Japan. I've been told it's a fascinating country. You'll love it.'

'And what about my business?' Kate enquired coolly. 'You seem very conveniently to have forgotten my commitments in your eagerness to sweep me off my feet.'

'That's where you're wrong. I've thought it all out, and I've spoken to Liz.'

Kate stared at him open-mouthed. The effrontery of his assumptions took her breath away as he went on, 'She's prepared to take overall charge, and until the second boutique gets going I'm prepared to help out with a manager's salary. I'll be able to afford it, after all,' he laughed, 'and then, when—if—we come back, you can take over again. And I dare say you can start up something in Tokyo, if you want something to occupy your time.' He smiled indulgently.

Kate got up slowly and backed away, hardly able to believe her ears.

'You've got it all worked out, haven't you? I forgive you for your little "mistake", you get your precious promotion, Liz gets the business, and I meekly agree to all this for the dubious privilege of marrying you—oh, and being allowed to run a little business just to keep me quiet.' She gave a brittle laugh. 'I ought to thank you, I suppose, for this preposterous proposal. At least I know where your real priorities lie, if I still needed convincing—and if *you* still need convincing, Michael, let me say now, once and finally, that nothing would persuade me to marry you, not if you were the last man on earth. And to think I imagined we really loved each other, once . . .'

Her voice broke then as she swung on her heel and stumbled along the darkened quay, tripping over coils of rope and mooring rings in her desperate urge to escape, running and running back to the sanctuary of her car.

CHAPTER NINE

IT ONLY occurred to Kate when she was nearly home that she had left Michael stranded in the village.

'Serve him right!' she muttered furiously. He was perfectly capable of finding a taxi, and if he'd lost her address it was just too bad. He could lose himself altogether for all she cared.

Once back home she locked and bolted the front door and turned out all the lights, then collapsed on to the nearest chair without the energy even to climb the stairs and go to bed. She wouldn't sleep, anyway, she knew that.

She must have fallen into a doze, though, for some time later she woke with a start as lights swept the front of the house and a car came crunching to a halt outside. Michael's taxi, presumably. Doors opened and shut and the car drove off again.

Kate held her breath. Michael would see her car and know she was there. Would he try to come in? Footsteps approached the door and paused, and Kate could almost see him standing there, one hand poised to knock—but nothing happened and after a moment the footsteps retreated and then a second car started up and moved off, down the track, taking him away and out of her life for ever.

She exhaled a long sigh. So that was that. She was too emotionally drained to feel any emotion—even relief. Enough that Michael's motives in coming to seek her out had been revealed in all their true colours. If he needed a wife, he could always take Carol to Tokyo—

she'd be happy enough to oblige him, again, Kate thought bitterly. They were welcome to one another.

Perhaps he'd never loved her, not really. Wanted her, yes, but was he even capable of feeling real, true love?

Had she sensed that all along, deep down? Was that why she had always refused to move in with him and insisted on maintaining what Michael had called her 'old-fashioned morality' to save herself for their wedding-night?

Kate shook her head wearily. There was no point in trying to analyse her feelings now, not when she was so tired, but one thing she was sure of, she realised with a sense of release. Michael no longer had the power to hurt her.

Slowly she got to her feet and went upstairs, pausing at the top to glance into the second bedroom which Alex had used earlier that evening so short a time ago, and yet how long it seemed since they had been together.

She went inside and turned on the light. He'd left the towel she'd lent him neatly folded up on a chair and almost without thinking what she was doing Kate went over and picked it up, holding it to her face and breathing in the faint, distinctive aroma that was his and which brought flooding over her, with shocking intensity, waves of longing to be back on that sunlit beach, naked and in his arms.

There had never been any question of holding anything back from Alex. She had given herself to him unhesitatingly, and if he was here now, and if he wanted her...

She sank on to the bed, still holding Alex's towel to her cheek as a child might clutch a familiar toy for comfort. He never would want her again, there was no reason why he should. She'd seen that in his face as he'd left her and Michael together. He thought...

Kate leapt to her feet as the realisation hit her. Alex thought that those 'regrets' she had spoken about had

been on account of Michael. That she'd regretted the
rift that had opened up between her and her fiancé—
after all, he'd known nothing about the supposed baby—
and, now that Michael had come looking for her, begging
her forgiveness, all their past misunderstandings would
be healed and the betrothal ring would once more be on
her finger.

What had Alex's parting words been? 'I won't stand
in your way.' How much more clearly could he have told
her what was in his mind? And now, no doubt, he was
picturing her—if he was thinking of her at all—back in
Michael's arms, even here, in this room, or in her bed.
And if she never saw him again he'd never know the
truth.

So what is the truth? a stern voice whispered within
her. Go on, confess it to yourself, if to no one else. You
owe him that much.

Kate wrapped her arms tightly round the towel and
buried her face in this tenuous link with the man whose
path had so fatefully crossed and become intertwined
with her own. The man she now knew without the
faintest shadow of a doubt that she loved, desperately
and totally.

Unlike Michael, he had never made any demands on
her nor even criticised her when she'd been at her most
prickly, her gentle, passionate knight errant. And she,
who had always prided herself on her independence and
resourcefulness, had strangely been only too glad to
accept his help and his sympathy.

She had confided so much in him but even now, after
all they had shared, she was scarcely any nearer knowing
what really lay behind that humorous, easy-going ex-
terior than she had been when they had first met in the
airport lounge. She had never discovered more than the
most superficial details of his work or his family because she had never asked, and the only time she had
tried to question him, about the mystery girl in the

photograph, he had headed her off so firmly that she'd never mentioned her again.

Small wonder he'd made his goodbye sound so final. He can't think I care for him at all, Kate told herself miserably, and I do, I do, so much.

The thought that she might never see him again was more than she could bear and tears welled up in her eyes and ran down her cheeks to drop on to Alex's towel. She held it to her face and whispered his name over and over again like an incantation.

'Alexandros...Alex, I love you...'

It didn't matter that they'd known one another barely a week. All she wanted, more than anything she'd ever wanted in the whole of her life, was to spend her life with him, giving herself to him, and discovering everything about him. Pride, independence, even her precious career, meant nothing—she would give them all up if she could just be with him.

Somehow she would have to convince him of her feelings. If only it were morning and she could go to find him!

Kate jumped up, still clutching her talisman, and ran downstairs again, too keyed up now even to try to sleep.

She made some coffee and prowled around the living-room like a caged animal trying to get her thoughts and emotions into some sort of order as she waited for the dawn.

Her eyes fell on the shelf of books and she seized the nearest one, a guide-book to Greece, and sat down to try to read it, but however hard she tried to concentrate on the descriptions of ancient palaces and temples it was impossible to take anything in, and at last her hand dropped the book on to the floor and she drifted off into a fitful sleep.

She woke, stiff and bleary-eyed, a few hours later when the grey light of dawn was just filtering through the trees outside. For a moment she couldn't think where she was or why she was so uncomfortable, then she remembered. Alex . . . and Michael . . .

She went up to the bathroom and splashed cold water over her face and neck before collecting up her cases which were still where Alex had put them the day before. Whatever happened, she didn't imagine she would be returning here again.

One last look round, then she locked the front door behind her for the last time and set off for Alex's village.

She had no clear idea of what she intended to do when she got there. It was still far too early to call at his house, but at least she would be there, within close reach of him. She would sit in the car and compose her thoughts so that when the time came she would be able to tell him what was in her mind—and heart—without stumbling. This was her last chance, ever, to get it right.

Kate drove down to the harbour and parked just a little way from Alex's house. There was no one stirring. All the houses were quiet and their curtains drawn and the fishing boats which had been out all night hadn't yet returned to their moorings.

The sea was a soft grey, unruffled by the faintest breeze, merging invisibly into the misty horizon. On any other day Kate would have sat marvelling at the view, but today she just felt sick with apprehension, knowing how much depended on her imminent interview with Alex, and her eyes remained fixed, almost unblinking, on his door.

She was sure he must be there. His car was parked outside and it was still too early for anyone to have given him a lift up to the hotel site.

Into her mind's eye slid a picture of him sleeping, unconscious of her waiting presence outside, and her body was racked with an agony of longing to be in his bed beside him, in his arms . . .

But he wasn't still sleeping. Even as she fought the tormenting image she saw his door open and Alex himself emerge, unshaven and dressed in old trainers, faded jeans and an old and shabby sweatshirt, torn at the hem.

The sight of his unkempt appearance told her more than any words could have done of the disturbed night be too must have spent. Why else was he up and about so early? Was he about to set off and come to find her?

She watched, holding her breath, as he paused by his car and slowly opened the door, but after a second's hesitation he frowned, shook his head and slammed the door to again. His hands plunged deep into his pockets as he strode away from her down the road towards the far end of the quay.

Now! Kate told herself. She must speak to him now, or it would be too late.

Her heart was pounding against her ribs as she slipped out of her car and closed the door quietly behind her, then began to run down the road towards Alex who had now stopped and was untying his neat, white boat.

'Alex!' Her voice came out as a kind of hoarse whisper, but she dared not shout. The last thing she wanted to do was wake the whole village. 'Alex!' she called again. 'Wait! There's something I want to tell you.'

Alex slewed round to face her, astonishment mingled on his dark face with some other emotion she couldn't quite make out at this distance, and although she hoped it might be pleasure she was assailed by terrible doubts that it more resembled dislike, if not actual hostility.

'What are you doing here?'

The chill in his voice stopped her abruptly in her tracks and his eyes, colourless and devoid of the least hint of warmth, flashed an unmistakable warning.

'So?'

Kate spread her hands in a helpless gesture which did nothing to disarm him.

'I wanted...that is,' she stammered, 'there's something I need to tell you. And something I want to know.'

Again she stopped as his mouth narrowed irritably.

'Well?'

Kate took a couple of steps nearer and saw his face close up to shut her out as effectively as if he'd gone back to his house and slammed the door shut on her.

'So what was it you've come to tell me? I'd be grateful if you'd get on with it. As you see, I'm about to take the boat out...'

He stooped to it and held the mooring rope lightly as though poised to jump aboard and sail away and out of Kate's life for ever.

She gazed miserably at him. What could she say in the face of such scorn?

'Let me help you,' he offered, his lips curling sardonically, 'as you are clearly having such difficulty finding the words. It's always embarrassing giving someone the brush-off, and I must say I do appreciate your taking the trouble to come and tell me—so early in the morning, too!'

'Tell you what?' It was Kate's turn to be astonished, but hardly reassured by the grimness of his tone.

'That it's been nice knowing me—at least, that was the impression you gave me,' Alex added with heavy irony as his eyes left her face to travel slowly down her body, lingering every now and again as though mentally stripping her clothes away to leave her as naked as she'd been the day before, in his arms.

'Alex,' she began, scarlet flooding her face and neck, 'I—— '

But Alex waved a peremptory hand as he went on in harsher tones, 'And now your fiancé's come back, and you've come to say goodbye. Well, I wish you both every happiness, Kate, and I'm glad everything's worked out for you after all. All forgiven and forgotten, is it?'

He gave the mooring rope a savage jerk which brought the boat bumping up to the low sea wall.

'You can forget all those "regrets" that have been tormenting you so much now, can't you? And just to put your mind completely at rest, I have no regrets either. Easy come, easy go...'

He shrugged and his mouth curved into a bitter smile which failed to reach his eyes. 'No hard feelings? Just a few pleasurable memories—and here's a final one to add to them.'

Still holding the rope in one hand, with the other he reached out and grabbed Kate's arm, pulling her hard up against his chest.

'Does Michael kiss you like this?'

His head came down with a swiftness that rocked her off balance and she felt his arm tighten mercilessly round her not so much in an embrace as to prevent her escape.

His mouth crushed hers with punishing force, stifling the breath from her lungs until she thought she was going to suffocate in his arms. At last he raised his head just enough to enable him to search her face with eyes cold as northern seas.

'Well,' he rasped, 'will you add that to your memories? And this?'

Kate gasped as his lips sought hers again, but now with a soft sensuousness that turned her legs to jelly and made the muscles of her stomach ache with a terrible longing she knew could never be assuaged. He kissed her mouth and her throat, careless of who might be watching, and at the same time his free hand relaxed its fierce hold and began to roam over her body, exploring and lingering on each curve in turn as though to remind himself of its contours and finally slipping up to curl round the nape of her neck beneath the heavy fall of chestnut hair.

'And where is he now, your fiancé?' Alex spat out the words with a venom of which Kate would never have thought him capable. 'Still in your bed, I presume.' His fingers tightened painfully. 'Does he know about your little escapade yesterday, or did you conveniently forget to mention it? Or maybe he's a tolerant sort of guy and doesn't care what his girl gets up to when he's away. But I can tell you this—if you were *my* girl I'd make sure I was the only one who ever made love to you. Does he know you're visiting yesterday's lover now, or is he under the illusion that you're merely taking a gentle morning stroll?'

Tears sprang to Kate's eyes, enlarging them into shining emerald pools as she gazed up at him, appalled.

'How can you be so cruel, Alex? It's not like you, and you've not given me a chance to explain. Michael and I——'

Alex dropped his arm and gave her a little push as though anxious to be rid of her. 'How do you know it's not like me? When have you ever bothered to find out what I'm like? I was just a convenient escort—and lover, too—once Maria and I had proved our usefulness by looking after you, and now, when it suits you, it's "Goodbye, Alex, and thanks but no thanks." I believe that's how the saying goes?' he ended with cutting flippancy.

He dropped his eyes to the rope still dangling from his hand, as though surprised to see it there.

'Hold this, would you? It's time I went.'

He flung rather than handed her the end of the rope as he jumped down into the boat and turned away to adjust the outboard motor.

Kate clung on to it as though it were her very lifeline. 'Alex, please, that's not——' she began, but the rest of her words were drowned by the sound of the engine starting up. For one reckless moment she contemplated jumping into the boat with Alex. At least then she could insist on making him listen to her, but even that last chance was denied her as he tugged the rope from her hands. Then, without another word, he pushed off from the sea wall, gave her a mocking wave and turned the boat out to sea.

Kate stood, transfixed by her helplessness, watching his slowly diminishing figure. If she had had any doubts about the depth of her love for him they were dispelled now, when it was too late and he was disappearing from her sight and out of her life for ever, and he would never know just how much she loved him. He would go on assuming she and Michael were back together, soon to be married and happy every after.

But why? What could have convinced him so strongly that all their differences had been sorted out?

She sat down on the wall, hugging her knees and staring at the small speck that was the boat carrying Alex further and further away.

If only she had had the courage to *make* him listen to her—but his sarcastic overriding of each of her attempts to tell him what was in her heart had been so out of character that she'd been rendered speechless.

A final agonised glance seawards told her he had vanished from sight round the headland across the bay and with infinite weariness she got to her feet and dragged herself back along the road towards her car.

As she paused momentarily outside Alex's house the front door opened and Maria emerged, her face, as she saw Kate, as vivid a picture of conflicting emotions as her brother's had been.

'Kate? What are you doing here so early?'

Kate smiled faintly. 'Trying to explain something to Alex, only he wasn't in a listening mood.'

Maria did not respond to Kate's smile and her face remained grave and anxious.

'He was very upset,' she said quietly. 'Ever since he got home yesterday evening he's hardly spoken. All I know is that it had something to do with you.'

The two girls stared miserably at one another, and Maria's expression softened fractionally. She stood aside and held the door open.

'You'd better come in,' she invited Kate. 'I don't know what's happened between you and Alex, but what I do know is that you're in no fit state to drive.

'You don't have to talk if you don't want to,' she told Kate a short while later as they were sitting at the kitchen table, a large pot of coffee between them. Kate sipped at her cup slowly, grateful for the warmth that slipped down her throat, and gazed at Maria despairingly.

'I think I'd like to explain—why I'm here, at any rate,' she said slowly. 'And maybe you could tell Alex some time. I couldn't bear it if he went on thinking as badly of me as he does now. He wouldn't give me a chance to speak. Just accused me...'

The words stuck in her throat, choking her, and she shook her head hopelessly.

'You're fond of him, aren't you?' Maria asked gently.

Kate nodded. 'But he doesn't know that. He thinks I've gone back to Michael.'

'Michael?' Maria sounded puzzled. 'Who's Michael?'

'I'd better begin at the beginning,' Kate sighed, 'if you've got time, that is?' She managed a wan smile and the other girl reached across and covered Kate's hand with hers.

'As long as it takes,' she assured her.

So Kate found herself telling Maria everything, not only about her relationship with Michael, their engagement and the reasons for its break-up.

'And there's something else, too,' Kate said finally, her voice low and colourless. 'Michael thought Carol was going to have a child—his child. Alex knows all the rest, but I couldn't bring myself to tell him about that. It was too humiliating and hurtful. Especially as...' Kate's voice became even bleaker, and she dropped her gaze to the floor as with tense little movements her fingers began plaiting the fringe on the tablecloth.

'You see, my father ran out on my mother as soon as I was born, and she just gave up. Oh, I know that lots of mothers can manage to bring up several children on their own. It's a struggle, but they cope. But not mine,' she added with a hollow laugh. 'We drifted about from bedsit to bedsit—and so-called "uncle" to "uncle". I won't go into it all, it's too sordid and humiliating, but eventually I was taken into care and I spent the rest of my childhood in a series of foster homes, some good, some not so good...'

Kate's eyes clouded as the words trailed away before she continued rather too brightly, 'So I've always shied away from the thought of having a family of my own. I didn't think I had the right inborn instincts in here——' She clenched her hand into a fist and struck herself on the chest. 'No experience of loving, you see— like parents, like child. The whole ghastly circle might begin all over again. I just couldn't take the risk.'

An unhappy silence fell between then, then Kate went on doggedly, 'But that's all in the past. It just helps to explain—oh, various things. Anyway, Michael came back here, yesterday, to find me and try to patch things up. He said his fling with Carol had meant nothing, that the baby had been a false alarm, and that he didn't mind about us not having children, but it was me he wanted, though not, as it turned out, because he loves me, but because his promotion depends on him having a wife.'

'And this was yesterday?' Maria asked quietly. 'Yesterday evening?'

Kate nodded dismally. 'He arrived after Alex and I got back.'

She coloured faintly, hoping Maria would not press her as to where they had returned from, and went on quickly, 'We were just about to go out for a meal, but Michael said what he had to tell me was too urgent to wait, so Alex left. But what I don't understand, Maria, is why he was so cruel to me just now. I came to tell him it's all over, for ever, between Michael and me, but he wouldn't even begin to listen, and accused me of...'

She bowed her head wearily to rest her chin on her linked hands. 'I don't think I want to remember what he accused me of, but it was all wrong, and now he'll never know...'

Again her voice drifted away into silence until Maria prompted her. 'Know what?'

'That I love him,' Kate replied brokenly. 'I realise it's only a few days ago that we met, but I *know* I love him. It's as simple as that, and if he asked me to stay on— again——' her mouth curved into a reminiscent smile '—I'd stay with him for ever. Only he won't, I know that, so I'll leave now before I make an even greater fool of myself than I have already.'

She pushed her chair back and smiled wanly at Maria. 'Thanks for listening, Maria. At least I've told someone, and whether you tell Alex or not, well, it's up to you. It won't make any difference one way or another now. He'll never change his opinion of me.'

She walked slowly to the door where she turned, frowning.

'There's just one thing I'd like to know, before I go. That evening you had the migraine and couldn't come to supper, when Alex came on his own...?'

Maria nodded, waiting for her to continue.

'Well, I was riled, I suppose, by something he said about the importance of families.' Kate blushed at the memory of her outburst, but she had to persevere and find out what it was that had so upset him, whatever the cost. This was her last chance.

'I asked him if he thought families were so important, how was it he hadn't got one of his own?'

There was a quick gasp that made Kate stare at Maria whose face had gone suddenly pale, as Alex's had done, Kate recalled with a sharp pang.

'If you said that, and he still went on seeing you, he must feel——' Maria broke off, shaking her head in disbelief. 'You obviously don't know him very well, or you'd never have asked him such a terrible thing.'

'Terrible?' Kate asked faintly.

'Alex was married, some years ago, to a lovely Scottish girl—dark and so pretty. Fiona, her name was. There's a photo of her over there . . .' Maria nodded towards the shelf.

'And in his wallet,' Kate whispered numbly as the blood rushed from her face.

'They were so happy—too happy, perhaps, I don't know.'

Maria spread her hands in a gesture of utter incomprehension. 'They had a baby, Nicholas——' Kate's gaze was drawn inexorably to the other photograph, the one of the happy family group and the little boy laughing down into his father's face, and closed her eyes in anguish as Maria continued, 'One day as she was driving back from a shopping trip Fiona's car was smashed into by a lorry. They were both killed instantly, she and Niko.'

She had no need to say any more.

Kate held on to the wall, feeling faint and sick. She couldn't have known, but all the same . . . The wonder was, as Maria had said, that Alex had gone on seeing her, let alone wanting to make love to her. And all the time he had told her nothing.

'He's never gone out with another girl since then,' Maria said quietly. 'Not until he met you.'

The two girls looked at one another helplessly, then Kate turned and opened the door.

'Thanks again for listening, and telling me about . . .' She spread her hands, unable to speak about the tragedy. 'I'm sorry, so very sorry. And if, some time, you do feel you could explain to Alex . . . ?'

'You could stay and explain everything yourself,' Maria suggested doubtfully, 'but, in all fairness to you, I think I should maybe mention something else.'

She fixed dark, troubled eyes on Kate's face, and Kate's heart sank even further, if that was possible.

'Go on.' The words were almost inaudible and Maria had visibly to steel herself to drive in the final nail in the coffin of Kate's hopes.

'He's always said, ever since the accident, that he would never marry again, however much he was attracted to any girl. I'm sorry, Kate, I really am, but I didn't want to raise any false hopes—and I'd no idea how you'd felt about him before today.'

'Nor had I,' Kate whispered as she finally fled the house. 'Nor had I, until it was too late.'

CHAPTER TEN

DELIBERATELY turning her eyes away from the sea and any possibility of catching so much as a fleeting glimpse of Alex, Kate flung herself into the car and tore away up the road, heedless of any other traffic she might meet coming down into the village.

Mercifully, there was nothing about, and she reached the main road safely, then, hardly knowing or caring where she was heading, she simply drove, on and on, to put as many kilometres between her and the Mani peninsula as she could before exhaustion finally set in.

Two almost sleepless nights she'd had, to say nothing of the emotional upheavals she had undergone over the past couple of days. Some rest this so-called holiday had turned out to be, Kate thought, with an inward burst of sardonic laughter. She'd have been far better off back home planning the new boutique, and how far away that seemed, and how she wished . . .

A blast on a car horn brought her up sharply as she realised with horror that she'd been drifting dangerously near the unprotected precipice on her right. The sight of a small roadside shrine reinforced the other driver's peremptory warning and simultaneously made her heart turn over on a wave of yearning as she remembered other shrines on the road where she'd had the accident that had brought Alex to her rescue and into her life again. Now, though, she was on her own, with no knight errant to come to her aid.

Pushing all such weakening thoughts firmly from her mind, Kate decided that the overriding priority at this precise moment was to find somewhere to stop for the night—anywhere, no matter how primitive, would do. All she needed right now was a bed and hours and hours of undisturbed sleep.

It was not long before she came to a signpost indicating some kind of village or hamlet up what was more like a track than a road leading away from the main highway. She could go on to the next town and find accommodation there, but some age-old animal instinct was urging her on to find somewhere secluded to hide away and nurse her wounds—some hole to curl up in where she couldn't be found, even should someone come looking for her.

'Thank goodness for the tourist industry,' Kate grinned wryly to herself some time later as she collapsed on to the clean, white bed in a tiny house at the end of the village street.

There hadn't been any kind of hotel, naturally enough, in this smallest of Greek mountain villages, but one or two residents had optimistically put 'Rent Rooms' signs in their windows, and Kate had settled for the least primitive-looking house to enquire at in her almost non-existent Greek.

Luckily her landlady, Mrs Kafopoulou, spoke a smattering of English, and obviously something in Kate's worn expression had touched her motherly heart, for with true Greek hospitality she had offered her coffee and sweets before showing her to her room.

'Later, some food?' she enquired kindly. 'No taverna here—you are...?'

The word 'hungry' clearly was not in her vocabulary and she patted her own ample stomach with a questioning smile at Kate who nodded gratefully.

'Yes, please. Thank you very much. First, though, I need a sleep.'

It could barely be called evening, but Mrs Kafopoulou did not appear to think Kate's request in any way odd, but nodded, still smiling, as she showed Kate up the narrow stairs to the little room at the back of her house.

'Is OK?' she asked anxiously, and Kate smiled gratefully.

'It's very OK—and thank you again.'

After a brief glance out of the window at the small back garden shaded by an ancient olive tree under which a dog lay, tethered and watchful, and hens scratched about, clucking comfortably, Kate kicked off her shoes and stretched out on the bed.

It was dark when a gentle tap on the door finally woke her and she sat up, blinking, wondering for a moment wherever she was.

The knock came again, and she remembered.

'Come in,' she called, switching on the bedside light.

Mrs Kafopoulou stood in the doorway holding a tray which she set down on the rickety chest of drawers against the wall.

'Food,' she explained, beaming. 'You sleep well?'

'Very well, thanks.' Kate swung her legs off the bed and sniffed eagerly. Whatever it was steaming away in the bowl Mrs Kafopoulou had brought her smelt delicious and she suddenly realised she was hugely hungry. 'And that looks marvellous!' she exclaimed with an unmistakable enthusiasm that made her hostess beam again before leaving Kate to her supper.

Kate eyed the stew—lamb, probably, she thought—as avidly as though she hadn't seen food for days, and in fact the last meal she had eaten was the one she'd shared with Michael . . . but that was something to blot out of her mind. Instead, she concentrated all her attention on the tray in front of her—Mrs Kafopoulou's stew, a salad and hunks of crumbly bread with a glass of water to wash it all down.

After she had returned the tray with renewed thanks to her landlady, she took a short stroll the length of the

village street and back then, after a rudimentary wash,
fell into bed and a deep and dreamless sleep.

The sun was well up and streaming into her room when
she woke the following morning, but Kate made no effort
to stir beyond settling her pillow more comfortably so
that she could watch the olive branches move gently
against the blue sky.

I could stay here for ever and ever, she thought lazily,
hidden away from the world with no worries to bother
me ever again. I could sell my flat and my half of the
business and use the proceeds to buy a little cottage here
miles from anywhere and do...what? Nothing, absolutely nothing.

Kate closed her eyes and smiled contentedly to herself.
There was no sound from downstairs and hardly any
from outside. She might be alone in the world apart from
the sparrows and hens she could just hear chattering
companionably to one another.

She needn't even get up if she didn't feel like it. She
was sure Mrs Kafopoulou wouldn't mind.

She must have dozed off again, for the sun had moved
round the next time she opened her eyes, leaving the
room in shadow. She looked at her watch and gasped.
Twelve o'clock! Surely it couldn't be?

When she got downstairs she found that Mrs
Kafopoulou had left a tray out for her with bread, an
orange and yogurt, with a jar of Nescafé on the side,
but of her landlady herself there was no sign. Obviously
she had decided to go about her own business and leave
her guest to her own devices.

Kate made herself a cup of coffee, ate the yogurt and
then, on a sudden impulse, wrapped the bread and
orange in a paper napkin and set off along the village
street and up into the hills. She followed the goat tracks
through the olive groves and scrub, not knowing where
they led, but just walking in the clean, herb-scented air,
her mind as blank as she could make it until, tired out,

she made her way home again to another of Mrs
Kafopoulou's delicious stews and the blessed oblivion
of sleep.

This became the pattern of her days—walking, eating
and sleeping, not daring to think about anything until
her scarred heart had begun to heal.

This was the rest Liz had wanted her to have, but not
exactly how she had planned it, Kate thought with a
private grin one day when she was sitting on a rocky
hillside munching a piece of bread.

She stretched back, leaning on her elbows and staring
out at the deserted landscape surrounding her. No sound,
except the occasional flute of a small bird somewhere in
the bushes disturbed the all-pervading peace and Kate
sensed that now, perhaps, she could let her thoughts me-
ander towards the two men whose unseen, unsettling
presences still needed exorcising.

About Michael she just felt a great sadness, for deep
down she recognised that he probably did really love her
in his own peculiarly twisted way.

Kate sat up and hugged her knees as she conjured up
his face in her mind, not angry and hurt as when she
had last seen it, but as she had known it for so many
years—strong, serious and tender, too.

He'd always been there to help and advise her, and
he'd been an interesting and amusing companion, she
couldn't deny that, even now. They had made the ideal
couple, or so all their friends had thought, so why had
she consistently prevaricated whenever he had tried to
pin her down to an actual date for their wedding? It
hadn't only been because of her business commitments,
as she had constantly asserted.

If Alex... Even as his name formed itself in her mind
her stomach lurched painfully, but she forced herself to
go on.

If Alex had asked her to marry him when she had lain
in his arms on that enchanted beach, wouldn't she have

accepted him there and then, unreservedly and
ecstatically?

How, she wondered wretchedly, could she have de-
ceived herself, and poor Michael, too, for so long into
thinking what she felt for him was the real, burning love
that in fact only Alex could kindle in her heart, her body
and her soul?

And, her conscience ruthlessly informed her, her re-
fusal to marry Michael had nothing whatever to do with
her unwillingness to have a family of her own.

Some instinct, buried deep in her subconscious, had
invented the excuse of her own inadequate and unhappy
childhood, but in truth it was something much simpler
than that which had made her shrink from the idea of
motherhood.

Michael was not the man she wanted as the father of
her children—nor as her lover; but how gladly she had
surrendered to Alex's lovemaking, never questioning nor
doubting the rightness of it. If he wanted her to give
him children... But that was not to be, now or ever.

Maria's words rang a death knell of her hopes. 'He's
always said he would never marry again.'

Neither she nor any other girl could replace his lost
wife and child, and the sooner she, Kate, put an end to
her impossible dreams, the better for her sanity and peace
of mind.

Maybe it was time now to go home, not to Mrs
Kafopoulou's little house, but to her own home and the
exciting business challenges awaiting her.

Slowly she got to her feet and stretched, flexing her
mental as well as her physical muscles, feeling a new
strength seep back into her as though she were recov-
ering from a virus—the virus of love, Kate thought fancifully with a rueful smile at her own expense. Well, so
be it. Recuperation might still be needed, but at least
the process had begun.

*   *   *

The following morning she said her grateful and affectionate farewell to Mrs Kafopoulou who seemed genuinely sorry to see her go.

'You are more happy now?' she smiled shyly, resting her hand on Kate's arm. 'You sleep well and eat well in my house, and now you are well.'

They both laughed.

'I am very well,' Kate assured her. 'And I have you to thank for that. You have been so kind to me.'

To her embarrassment the tears which since her arrival in Greece seemed to flow on the slightest provocation, welled up and threatened to trickle down her cheeks. Maybe her cure was not as complete as she had thought, and Mrs Kafopoulou only made matters worse as she linked her arm in Kate's to walk up the road to the car.

'A pretty girl like you needs a man—a husband.' She grinned mischievously. 'In Greek we use the same word for both. And you need children to stop the tears.'

She held Kate's hands and gazed thoughtfully up into her face for a moment. 'But I think they will not be long in coming,' she added softly. 'Then you will be truly happy.'

They said their final goodbyes and after promising to return as soon as she possibly could Kate set off, waving furiously until a curve in the road hid Mrs Kafopoulou from sight, and it wasn't until she had reached the main road again that she was assailed by the awful significance of her landlady's last words. And if she were right...?

Waves of alarm flooded through at the very thought.

She and Alex hadn't taken any sort of precautions, but surely, nothing could have happened...

'No!' she cried out loud. No, no. Mrs Kafopoulou was only fantasising in a kindly attempt to comfort her, not doing an early pregnancy test.

And yet weren't country women like her supposed to have a sixth sense where matters of life and death were concerned, and wasn't there, deep down in the most secret parts of her body, a grain of doubt, the sense of a seed beginning to burgeon...?

Supposing she were carrying Alex's child, after all her protestations that motherhood wasn't for her? She hardly dared think—or hope—that it might be so, but *if* she were...

No, no, no, she told herself again. It can't possibly be true. Nothing would result from that blissful afternoon—nothing!

It wasn't so easy, though, to blot out the possibility, however faint it might be, from her mind, and Kate was glad when she eventually drove into Navplion, a small but busy town where she had planned to spend a couple of nights on her way back to Athens. There were many ancient sites nearby and enough to do to take her mind off everything else for the time being at least.

First thing the next morning Kate set off, determined to see as many of the sites in the vicinity as she could fit in, beginning with the ancient theatre of Epidavros.

It was still early and there weren't many people about when she arrived and parked beneath the pine trees so, having equipped herself with a guide book from the kiosk, she wandered round, exploring the museum and the other buildings before following the well-beaten track to the most famous theatre of the ancient world.

Nothing she had read or seen in photographs had prepared her in the least for its spacious magnificence or the absolute perfection of its proportions. It was altogether wider, higher and more all-embracing than she could have imagined, and for a long while she just stood and drank it all in, heedless of the other tourists milling around her.

'Sorry!' A woman jostled her elbow accidentally, bringing her back to earth, and she smiled vaguely at her before moving on herself to watch curiously the little groups clustered round the circular stage where individuals were testing the astonishing acoustics of the place. Apparently even the sound of a coin being dropped was clearly audible in the very last, highest row of seats.

And it was true, Kate was delighted to discover a short time later as she sat in one of the topmost seats of all listening to the chink of distant coins and the amazing clarity of voices speaking so far below her.

The stone was warm in the sun and she closed her eyes, relaxing and trying to imagine herself centuries back in time watching a play and surrounded by the remote ancestors of people like Mrs Kafopoulou—and of Alex, too...

With infinite caution she let his image creep into the edges of her mind, startled and grateful too that she could think of him now without too much pain.

She remembered reading that this whole place had originally been a sanctuary dedicated to the healing of the sick, and maybe it wasn't too fanciful to imagine that perhaps there was still a benign presence here prepared to ease the suffering of any pilgrim who came seeking help.

Nonsense, Kate chided herself sternly, opening her eyes and giving herself a little shake. Superstitious nonsense, that was, and nothing more. Even so it was comforting, none the less, to think of all those thousands of people who had come here to look for and no doubt find, too, healing of body and mind.

She propped her elbows on her knees to cup her chin in her hands and gaze down at the crowds, noticing that someone was trying to persuade the other tourists to move away from the stage area, presumably keen to test the acoustics for himself.

Grumbling good-naturedly, they did as they were requested, leaving this one man in sole possession of the vital spot, a tall, dark man...

Kate blinked and her heart somersaulted so violently in her chest that she found herself clutching at it as though to keep it from leaping out of her body. Surely her eyes were deceiving her? It couldn't be Alex. It must be her over-active imagination playing cruel tricks.

She stood up, her eyes narrowed intently on that one solitary figure who had now turned and had lifted his head to scan the rows of seats, searching... searching, until he seemed to spot her silhouetted against the green backdrop of trees, and Kate swayed, collapsing dizzily back on to the stone seat. It *was* Alex, there was no doubt about it, but what could he be doing here—and was it actually her he was looking for?

Then, as clearly as though he were sitting in the next seat, she heard his voice.

'Kate, will you marry me?'

Now it wasn't only his eyes that were focused on her. She seemed to hear a concerted intake of breath as a sea of faces was turned in her direction and she knew that everyone within earshot was waiting eagerly for the next line in this drama unfolding so unexpectedly before them.

A few schoolchildren giggled, to be hushed by other bystanders, but Kate herself remained dumbstruck.

'How romantic!' a woman passing behind her exclaimed to her husband. 'Why couldn't you have proposed like that? Go on, love,' she urged Kate. 'Don't keep the poor man in suspense.'

Kate blushed at this unwelcome reminder of such concentrated interest in her, but her breath was coming in such uneven gasps that she knew it would be impossible to speak.

'Kate? Can you hear me?' Alex persisted, his own voice perhaps not quite so steady as it might have been— but that could have been just the effect of the place.

Shakily Kate got up again and nodded as she raised her hand in a tentative greeting.

'What's your answer, then? I love you, Kate, and I want you to be my wife and the mother of my children.'

The flush on Kate's cheeks deepened to a fiery scarlet and there were one or two embarrassed laughs from the people near her, but at least some of them were moving on now and Alex himself had relinquished his position centre-stage as he waited for her reply.

A crowd of sightseers hid him from view temporarily, and when next her anxious eyes caught sight of him he was striding purposefully towards the stairs between the rows of seats, climbing...climbing, all the time staring fixedly at her and still watched by a considerable number of their fascinated audience.

Clearly nothing less than an ecstatic acceptance of his proposal would satisfy them, and Kate had a strong suspicion that great applause would break out all round were she to fling herself into his arms and give them the happy ending they all wanted.

But the sight of Alex approaching her so determinedly drained her suddenly of all her will-power, and, now the moment that she had longed for so desperately and never thought would happen had arrived, she felt incapable of making any sort of decision, especially one so crucial.

Alex slowed as he neared her, but his eyes, glittering with an intensity that almost blinded her, never left her face.

'Kate,' he rasped in a low, harsh voice only she could hear now. 'I've found you.'

He held out his hand and almost shyly Kate put hers into it, feeling his fingers tighten convulsively round it as he drew her towards him.

'Come,' he said quietly. 'We can't talk here—but I meant what I said just now. Down there.'

He nodded towards the stage, the corners of his lips tilting with a hint of a smile that briefly lit his eyes with their old humour.

'I'm sorry if it embarrassed you, but it seemed the only way of making sure you didn't run away.'

Then, giving Kate no chance to respond one way or the other, he turned to lead her gently down the steps till they reached the ground where he slid his arm round her waist.

'I think we should find a less public spot than this, don't you?' he murmured somewhere above her studiously bent head. 'And a short walk will give you time to think over my proposal.'

The sound that emerged as Kate tried to speak was hardly more than an incomprehensible mumble, but Alex appeared not to worry as he guided her away from the theatre down a narrow path to a cluster of trees sheltering some fallen blocks of masonry.

'We can sit here,' he told her, loosing his hold of her to draw her down beside him on to a broad stone slab. ''And I can tell you...'

He broke off and looked away into the distance. 'There's so much I want to tell you—things I should have said before, when I had the chance.'

'And there are so many things I should have asked you,' Kate said softly.

Alex turned back quickly to face her, a gentle smile touching his lips. 'Do you know, that's the first time you've spoken.'

Kate nodded. 'I was so dazed I didn't know what to say.'

'About my proposal, or in general?'

'Either...both,' Kate replied helplessly. 'I thought we'd never meet again, and to see you, just now...and then when you said...asked me...' Her treacherous cheeks flushed again as the words trailed away into a silence charged with so many unspoken thoughts and emotions.

'How did you find me?' she asked at last. 'I didn't tell anybody where I was going. In fact, I didn't know myself. I just drove. I don't even know where I've been, in fact,' she added with a little laugh. 'I stayed in a tiny village somewhere in the hills, but I've no idea what its name was.'

Alex took her hand and played idly with her fingers. 'The only clue I had was the guidebook in your cottage. You'd left it open at the page describing Epidavros.'

'But that was pure chance!' Kate exclaimed in horror. 'I never planned to come here, not then. I'd only picked the book up to try and take my mind off——' She paused, and Alex supplied the missing words for her.

'Off me, or Michael, or maybe the two of us?'

Kate nodded slowly. 'Something like that.'

Again the silence settled round them, disturbed only by the remote sound of voices as the recollection of that sleepless night came flooding back—the revelation about Michael and his twisted motives for wanting to marry her, and the blinding realisation of her love for Alex followed by their dreadful confrontation the following morning.

And now he was here. Something, or someone— Maria, presumably, had changed his mind about her, but not, surely about marrying, in spite of his proposal made so publicly. That couldn't have been serious, just a way of attracting her attention.

Gently she withdrew her hand from his grasp and edged away from him on their unyielding seat. Instinct told her that even the slightest physical contact might only too easily sap the strength of mind she needed to ask the questions to which she needed such vital answers.

'What's made you change your mind about me?' She turned to Alex as she spoke and fixed him with wide green eyes. 'Why did you come looking for me, after all you said...?'

Her throat constricted and she allowed the words to remain unspoken as she watched a shadow briefly cross the dark, handsome face.

'Maria told me,' he said simply. 'She explained about what happened between you and Michael—everything.'

He didn't tell her of the battle his sister had fought to make him listen to her at all. His first reaction had been that nothing Kate had had to say either to him or to Maria was of the least interest to him, nor could any of it be trusted, but Maria had insisted, finally persuading him that Kate's story was true from beginning to end.

'You see,' he went on slowly, 'I drove up to your cottage that evening—late. I thought Michael would have left by then, and you might need a shoulder to cry on...'

He raised his eyes briefly with a dry smile and Kate opened her mouth to say something, but he made a gesture with his hand that warned her not to interrupt.

'There were two cars parked together outside, yours and his. And all the lights were out.'

Those two bald sentences told Kate everything.

'And you thought Michael...Michael and I...' she blurted out, 'that we'd resolved our differences——'

'And were cementing your new-found happiness,' Alex finished with a harshness that made Kate wince. 'Something like that. And after all that you and I had shared only hours before——'

He sprang up and began pacing up and down in front of her as he relived his own private agony and Kate watched, feeling powerless to help him yet at the same time unutterably relieved that he now knew how wrong his assumptions had been.

'I couldn't believe, you see, that you could be so devious or so fickle,' he burst out. 'And yet, what else could I think, with the evidence there before me? Then, when I saw you the next morning, I thought you'd come to tell me you were going back to him, and I just couldn't bear the thought of even hearing those words,' he ended in a low, almost inaudible voice.

He faced her now and crouched down in front of her, taking her hands back into his warm, firm grasp.

'If all we had been having was nothing more than a holiday flirtation I'd have been piqued, sure, but able to shrug off the whole thing and put it down to experience.' His eyes grew grave as he gazed into hers as though searching for something which he still remained unsure whether he would find. 'I have to be grateful to your Michael for one thing at least,' he commented wryly, his lips curving into a faint, self-deprecating smile. 'He convinced me, if I'd needed convincing, that it wasn't just a passing fancy, what I felt for you.'

He rose to his feet again and pulled her after him so that they stood facing one another beneath the pines, oblivious of anyone who might have been passing.

'Standing there, thinking of you in his arms as you'd been in mine, I hated him more than I'd ever have thought it possible to hate any man. I actually think I might have tried to kill him if he'd come out at that moment, because I realised then that I loved you, Kate, with all my soul and with all my body, too. You are a very beautiful and utterly desirable woman, and I want you with me always.'

Even as Kate's fingers tightened round his, a surge of despair swept over her. That proposal made so publicly from the stage of the ancient theatre had not been seriously meant. It was as she had suspected all along— simply a way of getting her to listen to him. Above all things she must heed Maria's warning about her brother's determination never to marry again.

But could she settle for anything less? She tilted her face towards him, but no sound came from her softly parted lips save an incoherent cry as his mouth came down to claim them.

'What would you have done if I hadn't been here?' she asked rather unsteadily when Alex eventually let her speak. 'You might have waited for ever for me to appear, and all the time I could have been miles away, maybe thousands, if I'd already flown home.'

She shuddered at the prospect, and Alex's arms tightened round her.

'I was going to give it another day, then, if you still hadn't shown up, I was going on to Athens to see if I could discover which flight you would be on, and I'd have followed you to England if necessary.'

'But it wasn't, was it?' Kate nestled back against his shoulder, gasping as his hand slid up her body to touch her breast and she turned to bury her face in his chest, feeling his heart pounding against her ear almost as wildly as her own was doing.

'There's something you haven't told me yet,' Alex reminded her softly. 'I did make a proposal just now, and I've come a long way to find the answer.'

Which proposal, he did not elucidate, and Kate's spirits felt like lead as she forced herself to disengage herself from his embrace to move away and search his face with anguished eyes.

'I'm not sure which proposal you need an answer to—and if you really meant them. Either of them.'

'Either? There was only one, surely, when I asked you to marry me.'

'Wasn't that just to make me listen to you? Afterwards, you said you wanted me to be with you always, and they don't necessarily mean the same,' Kate blurted out with a sad little smile. 'You see, Maria told me about what happened—your wife, Fiona, and your little boy. Oh, Alex, I am so sorry. I can't imagine anything more terrible happening to anybody, and I quite understand you never wanting to get married again. But I don't think I could settle for just an affair, however long-lasting. I need something permanent,' she ended dismally, sensing she'd probably signed the death warrant of her love.

There was a long silence and Kate stared at the ground, imprinting the patterns made by the fallen pine needles for ever on to her brain then, as though from a great distance, she heard Alex speak, his voice quieter and more serious than she had ever known it.

'When Fiona and Niko died, I thought my world had come to an end, and even the idea that it might be possible to fall in love again was anathema to me. It would be a betrayal, or so I thought. But I was wrong. As the cliché has it, time really does heal. And now, after so long, I have found another girl to love.'

Again he fell silent, and Kate held her breath as she waited for him to continue, which he did after a long, racking sigh.

'Those other loves can't be replaced, but marriage to this other girl, a lifetime spent together with her, would be different. Different and wonderful, too, but in its own way. Do you see?'

Kate nodded slowly and the eyes she raised to his face shone not just with tears but with a new and growing understanding which erupted into an inexpressible joy.

'So, my dearest love, I'll ask you again here, and privately—unless you'd like to give our audience a repeat performance?'

Kate shook her head.

'Will you marry me, Kate, and make me the happiest man on earth? And before you answer,' he went on quickly, his eyes alight with laughter as he put a finger against her lips, 'I want you to know that if you should want to wear shorts in public, that's fine by me.'

Kate stared at him in astonishment, wondering whatever he was talking about, then her cheeks coloured with embarrassment as she remembered her outburst that evening he'd come to dinner.

She opened her mouth, but before she could say anything Alex went on, his expression matching a new gravity in his tone, 'And there would be no way I'd want you to sacrifice your independence, or your career. It's you I want, as you are, and if you want to keep your business I'll even share you with it, if that's a condition of you becoming my wife.'

Even as Alex was speaking, Kate realised that for her the world of commerce, with all its wheeling and dealing, and its challenges, too, was beginning to lose its attraction. Until now her whole life had been centred on her career and making her business a success, but suddenly all that had been so important to her seemed a million miles away as she melted against his strong body, wrapping her arms round him to bring his head down to hers, but before she could give him her answer he pushed her gently away from him to search her face with a deep tenderness that made her catch her breath.

'There's something else,' he began quietly. 'If you really feel you don't want to have a family, I won't——'

But Kate shook her head, her eyes bright with unshed tears, as shyly she took his hand and laid it against her stomach.

'It's too late,' she whispered. 'I think we already...'

She heard a quick intake of breath and flung herself back into his arms with an incoherent cry muffled against his heart.

'Oh, my love,' Alex breathed. 'My dearest, dearest love.'

'As for the business,' Kate said unsteadily after several long minutes when she couldn't have spoken even had she wanted to, 'I don't think I'll have much time over the next few years to continue with anything like that. Liz can run the whole thing if she wants to, or I'll sell up. We'll have to see.'

Alex pressed his mouth to hers. 'I can't think what you mean,' he said after a moment.

'If I'm right, about the baby, it'll want brothers and sisters, won't it?' She blushed furiously. 'And they won't

HARLEQUIN ✦ PRESENTS®

A Year
DOWN UNDER

In 1993, Harlequin Presents celebrates the land down
under. In June, let us take you to the Australian Outback,
in OUTBACK MAN by Miranda Lee,
Harlequin Presents #1562.

Surviving a plane crash in the Australian Outback is
surely enough trauma to endure. So why does Adrianna
have to be rescued by Bryce McLean, a man so gorgeous
that he turns all her cherished beliefs upside-down? But
the desert proves to be an intimate and seductive setting
and suddenly Adrianna's only realities are the red-hot
dust *and* Bryce....

Share the adventure—and the romance—
of A Year Down Under!

Available this month in
A YEAR DOWN UNDER

SECRET ADMIRER
by Susan Napier
Harlequin Presents #1554
Wherever Harlequin books are sold.

YDU-MY

THREE UNFORGETTABLE HEROINES
THREE AWARD-WINNING AUTHORS

Untamed

MAVERICK HEARTS

A unique collection of historical short stories that capture the spirit of America's last frontier.

HEATHER GRAHAM POZZESSERE—over 10 million copies of her books in print worldwide
Lonesome Rider—The story of an Eastern widow and the renegade half-breed who becomes her protector.

PATRICIA POTTER—an author whose books are consistently Waldenbooks bestsellers
Against the Wind—Two people, battered by heartache, prove that love can heal all.

JOAN JOHNSTON—award-winning Western historical author with 17 books to her credit
One Simple Wish—A woman with a past discovers that dreams really do come true.

Join us for an exciting journey West with
UNTAMED
Available in July, wherever Harlequin books are sold.

MAV93

New York Times Bestselling Author

Sandra Brown

Tomorrow's Promise

**She cherished the memory
of love but was consumed
by a new passion too
fierce to ignore.**

For Keely Preston, the memory of her husband
Mark has been frozen in time since the day he was
listed as missing in action. And now, twelve years
later, twenty-six men listed as MIA have been
found.

Keely's torn between hope for Mark and despair
for herself. Because now, after all the years of
waiting, she has met another man!

**Don't miss TOMORROW'S PROMISE by
SANDRA BROWN.**

**Available in June wherever Harlequin
books are sold.**

TP

Where do you find hot Texas nights, smooth Texas charm,
and dangerously sexy cowboys?

Crystal Creek

WHITE LIGHTNING

by Sharon Brondos

Back a winner—Texas style!

Lynn McKinney knows Lightning is a winner and she is
totally committed to his training, despite her feud with her
investors. All she needs is time to prove she's right. But
once business partner Dr. Sam Townsend arrives on the
scene, Lynn realizes time is about to run out!

CRYSTAL CREEK reverberates with the exciting rhythm of
Texas. Each story features the rugged individuals who live
and love in the Lone Star State. And each one ends with
the same invitation...

Y'ALL COME BACK...REAL SOON!

Don't miss WHITE LIGHTNING by Sharon Brondos.
Available in June wherever Harlequin books are sold.

If you missed #82513 *Deep in the Heart*, #82514 *Cowboys and Cabernet* or #82515 *Amarillo
by Morning* and would like to order them, send your name, address, zip or postal code along
with a check or money order for $3.99 for each book ordered (do not send cash), plus 75¢
($1.00 in Canada) for postage and handling, payable to Harlequin Reader Service, to:

In the U.S.	In Canada
3010 Walden Avenue	P.O. Box 609
P.O. Box 1325	Fort Erie, Ontario
Buffalo, NY 14269-1325	L2A 5X3

Please specify book title(s) with your order.
Canadian residents add applicable federal and provincial taxes.

CC-4